W9-DCL-776

BORZOI BOOKS FOR YOUNG PEOPLE

Selected by

PHYLLIS R. FENNER

TIME TO LAUGH: *Funny Tales from Here and There*

Illustrated by Henry C. Pitz

GIANTS AND WITCHES AND A DRAGON OR TWO

Illustrated by Henry C. Pitz

PRINCESSES AND PEASANT BOYS:
Tales of Enchantment

Illustrated by Henry C. Pitz

ADVENTURE: *Rare and Magical*

Illustrated by Henry C. Pitz

FOOLS AND FUNNY FELLOWS:
More "Time To Laugh" Tales

Illustrated by Henry C. Pitz

GIGGLE BOX: *Funny Stories for Boys and Girls*

Illustrated by William Steig

MAGIC HOOFS: *Horse Stories from Many Lands*
(Originally published as THERE WAS A HORSE)

Illustrated by Henry C. Pitz

YANKEE DOODLE: *Stories of the Brave and the Free*

Illustrated by John Alan Maxwell

CRACK OF THE BAT: *Stories of Baseball*

STORIES OF THE SEA

Illustrated by Kurt Werth

CIRCUS PARADE: *Stories of the Big Top*

Illustrated by Lee Ames

Published by Alfred A. Knopf

Feasts and Frolics

SPECIAL STORIES FOR SPECIAL DAYS

°[Special Stories For Special Days]°

FEASTS
and
FROLICS

Selected by

PHYLLIS R. FENNER

Illustrated by Helen R. Durney

ALFRED·A·KNOPF: *NEW YORK*

1957

KEENE TEACHERS COLL
LIBRARY

C.H
2.10

32767
12/3/58

THE TINKER AND THE GHOST, copyright 1936 by Longmans, Green and Co.
ARCHIE AND THE APRIL FOOLS, copyright 1942 by Child Life.
THE BUNNY FACE, copyright 1944 by Mildred Jordan.
INDEPENDENCE DAY, copyright 1933 by Harper & Brothers.
THE MAGIC BALL, copyright 1924 by Doubleday & Company, Inc.
CHRISTMAS CHERRIES, copyright 1941 by Story Parade, Inc.
THE GENERAL DID WRONG, copyright 1949 by Story Parade, Inc.
CHRISTMAS IN SUMMER, copyright 1945 by Child Life.
CANDLES AT MIDNIGHT, copyright 1947 by Alice Geer Kelsey.
GIFTS FOR THE FIRST BIRTHDAY, copyright (under the title of *The Trapper's Tale*)
1916 by Harper & Brothers, copyright 1944 by Ruth Sawyer Durand.
THE TRUCE OF THE WOLF, copyright 1931 by Harcourt, Brace and Company, Inc.
THE PEDDLER OF BALLAGHADEREEN, copyright 1942 by Ruth Sawyer.
HENRY'S LINCOLN, copyright 1945 by Louise A. Neyhart.

Juv
PZ
5
.F35
Fe
1949

OCLC# 471217

THIS IS A BORZOI BOOK
PUBLISHED BY ALFRED A. KNOPF, INC.

Copyright 1949 by Alfred A. Knopf, Inc. No part of this book may be reproduced in any form without permission in writing from the original publisher of the volumes from which the individual stories have been taken (see Acknowledgment, page 159), except by a reviewer who may quote brief passages and reproduce not more than three illustrations in a review to be printed in a magazine or newspaper. Manufactured in the United States of America. Published simultaneously in Canada by Mc-Clelland & Stewart Limited.

Published September 19, 1949.
Second Printing, August 1950
Third Printing, December 1952
Fourth Printing, August 1957

ESPECIALLY FOR
Jessamine
WHO CELEBRATES THE
Fourth of July
FOR TWO REASONS

Every Day a Holiday

It is wonderful to look on the calendar and see some of the dates written in red. Those are very special days, Red Letter Days, either holidays or holy days. It is wonderful, too, when these days come right in the midst of a tiresome all-the-days-alike kind of week. They are bright spots, like something with a searchlight on it, and each spot has a meaning all its own.

We shoot off firecrackers (not as disastrously as the Peterkins, I hope), put out the flag, eat cakes with red cherries on them, or read, with deep seriousness, the Gettysburg Address, put on costumes and shiver with delight at the thought of a ghost or witch, wear a green tie, or sing carols, all according to the kind of day it is.

How would you like to have a holiday every day in the year, or at least, on any day you chose? Some morning wake up and think, "What fun it would be if it were Thanksgiving"; or again, "If it were only Easter"; or, "If only it were April 1st so I could fool someone." * Whenever you wish to celebrate a special day just read a story about it, and presto, you are carried away to a different world and atmosphere.

There are some days that are not in red at all, and yet they are special. When it is raining and you have to stay in, or at that quiet time just before going to bed, or when the family is around the fire together, how nice to have a story good enough to be read again and again.

In this book you will find many special days celebrated with stories, and they are so good you will not only read them on the special days but you will like them *every day in the year*.

Let's celebrate with a story!

P.F.

* Watch out—you may be fooled in this book.

Contents

Feasts and Frolics

SPECIAL STORIES FOR SPECIAL DAYS

The Tinker and the Ghost

'someone who mends household metal utensils, for example pots, pans.'

⁰₈⟦ *Ralph S. Boggs and Mary Gould Davis* ⟧₈⁰

Ohio

On the wide plain not far from the city of Toledo there once stood a great gray Castle. For many years before this story begins no one had dwelt there, because the Castle was haunted. There was no living soul within its walls, and yet on almost every night in the year a thin, sad voice moaned and wept and wailed through the huge, empty rooms. And on all Hallow's Eve a ghostly light appeared in the chimney, a light that flared and died and flared again against the dark sky.

Learned doctors and brave adventurers had tried to exorcise

3

the ghost. And the next morning they had been found in the great hall of the Castle, sitting lifeless before the empty fireplace.

Now one day in late October there came to the little village that nestled around the Castle walls a brave and jolly tinker whose name was Esteban. And while he sat in the market place mending the pots and pans the good wives told him about the haunted Castle. It was All Hallow's Eve, they said, and if he would wait until nightfall he could see the strange, ghostly light flare up from the chimney. He might, if he dared go near enough, hear the thin, sad voice echo through the silent rooms.

"If I dare!" Esteban repeated scornfully. "You must know, good wives, that I—Esteban—fear nothing, neither ghost nor human. I will gladly sleep in the Castle tonight, and keep this dismal spirit company."

The good wives looked at him in amazement. Did Esteban know that if he succeeded in banishing the ghost the owner of the Castle would give him a thousand gold reales? _gold pieces_

Esteban chuckled. If that was how matters stood, he would go to the Castle at nightfall and do his best to get rid of the thing that haunted it. But he was a man who liked plenty to eat and drink and a fire to keep him company. They must bring to him a load of faggots _wood_, a side of bacon, a flask of wine, a dozen fresh eggs and a frying pan. This the good wives gladly did. And as the dusk fell, Esteban loaded these things on the donkey's back and set out for the Castle. And you may be very sure that not one of the village people went very far along the way with him!

It was a dark night with a chill wind blowing and a hint of rain in the air. Esteban unsaddled his donkey and set him to graze on the short grass of the deserted courtyard. Then he carried his food and his faggots _wood_ into the great hall. It was dark as pitch there. Bats beat their soft wings in his face, and the air felt cold and musty. He lost no time in piling some of his faggots _wood_ in one corner of the huge stone fireplace and in lighting them _it_. As the red and golden flames leaped up the chimney Esteban rubbed his hands. Then he settled himself comfortably on the hearth.

"*That* is the thing to keep off both cold and fear," he said.

Carefully slicing some bacon he laid it in the pan and set it over the flames. How good it smelled! And how cheerful the sound of its crisp sizzling!

He had just lifted his flask to take a deep drink of the good wine when down the chimney there came a voice—a thin, sad voice—and "*Oh me!*" it wailed, "*Oh me! Oh me!*"

Esteban swallowed the wine and set the flask carefully down beside him.

"Not a very cheerful greeting, my friend," he said, as he moved the bacon on the pan so that it should be equally brown in all its parts. "But bearable to a man who is used to the braying of his donkey."

And, "*Oh me!*" sobbed the voice. "*Oh me! Oh me!*"

Esteban lifted the bacon carefully from the hot fat and laid it on a bit of brown paper to drain. Then he broke an egg into the frying pan. As he gently shook the pan so that the edges of his egg should be crisp and brown and the yolk soft, the voice came again. Only this time it was shrill and frightened.

"*Look out below,*" it called. "*I'm falling!*"

"All right," answered Esteban, "only don't fall into the frying pan."

With that there was a thump, and there on the hearth lay a man's leg! It was a good leg enough and it was clothed in the half of a pair of brown corduroy trousers.

Esteban ate his egg, a piece of bacon and drank again from the flask of wine. The wind howled around the Castle and the rain beat against the windows.

Then, "*Look out below,*" called the voice sharply. "*I'm falling!*"

There was a thump, and on the hearth there lay a second leg, just like the first!

Esteban moved it away from the fire and piled on more faggots. Then he warmed the fat in the frying pan and broke into it a second egg.

And, *"Look out below!"* roared the voice. And now it was no longer thin, but strong and lusty. *"Look out below! I'm falling!"*

"Fall away," Esteban answered cheerfully. "Only don't spill my egg."

There was a thump, heavier than the first two, and on the hearth there lay a trunk. It was clothed in a blue shirt and a brown corduroy coat.

Esteban was eating his third egg and the last of the cooked bacon when the voice called again, and down fell first one arm and then the other.

"Now," thought Esteban, as he put the frying pan on the fire and began to cook more bacon. "Now there is only the head. I confess that I am rather curious to see the head."

And: "LOOK OUT BELOW!" thundered the voice. "I'M FALLING—FALLING!"

And down the chimney there came tumbling a head!

It was a good head enough, with thick black hair, a long black beard and dark eyes that looked a little strained and anxious. Esteban's bacon was only half cooked. Nevertheless, he removed the pan from the fire and laid it on the hearth. And it is a good thing that he did, because before his eyes the parts of the body joined together, and a living man—or his ghost—stood before him! And *that* was a sight that might have startled Esteban into burning his fingers with the bacon fat.

"Good evening," said Esteban. "Will you have an egg and a bit of bacon?"

"No, I want no food," the ghost answered. "But I will tell you this, right here and now. You are the only man, out of all those who have come to the Castle, to stay here until I could get my body together again. The others died of sheer fright before I was half finished."

"That is because they did not have sense enough to bring food and fire with them," Esteban replied coolly. And he turned back to his frying pan.

"Wait a minute!" pleaded the ghost. "If you will help me a bit more, you will save my soul and get me into the Kingdom of Heaven. Out in the Courtyard, under a cypress tree, there are buried three bags—one of copper coins, one of silver coins, and one of gold coins. I stole them from some thieves and brought them here to the Castle to hide. But no sooner did I have them buried than the thieves overtook me, murdered me and cut my body into pieces. But they did not find the coins. Now you come with me and dig them up. Give the copper coins to the Church, the silver coins to the poor, and keep the gold coins for yourself. Then I will have expiated my sins and can go to the Kingdom of Heaven."

This suited Esteban. So he went out into the courtyard with the ghost. And you should have heard how the donkey brayed when he saw them!

When they reached the cypress tree in a corner of the courtyard: "Dig," said the ghost.

"Dig yourself," answered Esteban.

So the ghost dug, and after a time the three bags of money appeared.

"Now will you promise to do just what I asked you to do?" asked the ghost.

"Yes, I promise," Esteban answered.

"Then," said the Ghost, "strip my garments from me."

This Esteban did, and instantly the ghost disappeared, leaving his clothes lying there on the short grass of the courtyard. It went straight up to Heaven and knocked on the Gate. St. Peter opened it, and when the spirit explained that he had expiated his sins, gave him a cordial welcome.

Esteban carried the coins into the great hall of the castle, fried and ate another egg and then went peacefully to sleep before the fire.

The next morning when the village people came to carry away Esteban's body, they found him making an omelette out of the last of the fresh eggs.

"Are you alive?" they gasped.

"I am," Esteban answered. "And the food and the faggots lasted through very nicely. Now I will go to the owner of the Castle and collect my thousand gold reales. The ghost has gone for good and all. You will find his clothes lying out in the courtyard."

And before their astonished eyes he loaded the bags of coins on the donkey's back and departed.

First he collected the thousand gold reales from the grateful lord of the Castle. Then he returned to Toledo, gave the copper coins to the cura of his church, and faithfully distributed the silver ones among the poor. And on the thousand reales and the golden coins he lived in idleness and a great contentment for many years.

Archie and the April Fools

∘⟦ *B. J. Chute* ⟧∘

"Ted," said Jimmy Brewster, coming into the living room rather suddenly, "I hate to mention it, but there's a giraffe in the back yard."

His brother roused himself from the study of a photograph, gave Jimmy a puzzled look, then glanced at the calendar. A peaceful smile dawned upon his face. The calendar unquestionably proclaimed the fact that it was April first.

"Run away, my good man," said Ted. "I'm busy. You know, Jimmy, there's definitely a light leak in our camera. We've certainly got to get a new one, as soon as we have enough money."

"We're going to get a projector," Jimmy reminded him, "and, while I hate to mention it again, there *is* a giraffe in our back yard."

"I know, I know. And there's a baby hippopotamus in the kitchen sink, too, but don't bother me with that now. Just put April Fool's Day out of your mind." Ted sighed. "What kind of camera do you think we should get?"

"Projector," said Jimmy, gazing thoughtfully out the window. "I take it all back. There *isn't* a giraffe in the back yard."

Ted said, "That's better. You can't catch me on those old April Fool gags."

"He isn't in the back yard," said Jimmy, "because now he's in the side yard."

Ted fixed his brother with a glittering eye. "Now look here, you poor cluck, enough's enough. Once is funny, but—" he broke off, his gaze drawn to the window by Jimmy's intent stare, and made a noise like a drowning suction pump.

"You see?" said Jimmy reproachfully.

Ted saw. He rushed to the window and peered out wildly. Jimmy nodded in sympathy. He knew how Ted felt. But there was no getting away from it—the large spotted object in the Brewster peony bed *was* a giraffe.

"I hope," said Jimmy, with dignity, "that this will be a lesson to you to trust me. I was deeply hurt—"

"Stop babbling," Ted requested, recovering slightly. "What are we going to do about this—this monster?"

Jimmy gazed out at the giraffe, which had left the peony bed and was munching a convenient tree, its head out of sight and its long thin neck looking like a large spotted serpent. "I read a book once," said Jimmy.

"This is no time to discuss your literary exploits," his brother told him fiercely. "Great howling buttercups! We've got to *do* something."

"This book," said Jimmy, undiscouraged, "said that giraffes can run faster than most horses."

"Yoicks! We've got to catch him. He probably belongs to the zoo."

"Maybe it would be better just to leave him alone," said Jimmy. "The book also said they kick with their hind legs, and, while naturally gentle, are capable of making a stout resistance."

Ted, who had been about to leave the house and organize a giraffe hunt, stopped in his tracks. "Stout resistance, huh? Perhaps we'd better call the zoo first."

"You watch the giraffe, and I'll call 'em." Jimmy grabbed for the phone book. "Circle 2-0123. Hurry, operator. . . . Hello, hello. Look, this is Jimmy Brewster, out on the Pine Road. We've got a giraffe here . . . A GIRAFFE. One of those things from Africa with long necks. . . . I want your what? Your accounting department? I do *not* want your accounting department. I want—" He broke off suddenly. "Look, what number is this? . . . Oh. Oh, I see. I'm sorry." He hung up, rather sadly. "That was the bank. They said I wanted their accounting department."

"Get going," Ted advised. "He's eating the lilac bush now."

"Circle 2-0123," Jimmy said again into the phone. "Ted, if you were a bank, would you refer a giraffe to your accounting department? . . . Hello. Is this the zoo? . . . Well, have you lost a giraffe? Yes. Yes? You have? . . . Well, it's here in our peony bed."

"Lilac," said Ted.

"Lilac bed," Jimmy corrected himself. "What do you want us to do?" There followed a brief, rather one-sided conversation, then Jimmy said, "Thank you. Yes, sure, we will," and hung up.

"What'd they say?"

"It belongs to the zoo all right. They're sending men out with a truck, and we're to keep the giraffe here until they come." He paused. "Ted, there's a twenty-five dollar reward for the thing. He said we'd get it, if we caught the giraffe."

"Zowie!" Ted shouted. "We can get that camera."

"Projector," said Jimmy automatically.

"Camera," said Ted. "All we have to do—" He stopped short. "Faster than a horse, huh? Suppose it runs away when it sees us? Maybe it's scared of people."

"Frankly," said Jimmy, "that would make it unanimous. I'm scared of it."

Ted waved his hand airily. "Don't be difficult. Look, you go and get the encyclopedia and see what it says about giraffes, while I watch the beast out the window."

Jimmy dashed off and returned with the required volume. Ted, who had been watching the giraffe anxiously, said, "One of the advantages of living in the country is there's plenty of giraffe food around. He's eating the ivy now. Mother and Dad won't be pleased."

"Well, if they were home," said Jimmy reasonably, "they could tell Archie so."

"Archie?"

"That's his name. The zoo man told me." He began to read. "The giraffe or camelopard—good night, is that what he is? A camelopard!"

"Go *on*," said Ted.

Jimmy went on. "Native of Africa—occurs generally in herds of from five to forty. Whoops! Not here, I hope. Feeds on leaves and small branches of trees. Yes, we'd guessed that. Seven vertebrae in neck. Hey! That's all *I've* got. It hardly seems fair. Look at the length of his neck compared to mine."

"If you don't get a move on," Ted warned him dangerously, "there won't be any Archie here to have a neck."

Jimmy read on hastily. "No vocal chords—well, anyway he can't answer back then . . . Generally seeks safety in flight. That's not so good . . . Large, clear eyes. Nice for Archie, but no use to us. Ah, here we are!"

"About time," said Ted bitterly.

"What I said about their kicking with their hind legs," said Jimmy, "is true. But it seems they only kick lions."

"What do you mean, they only kick lions?"

"Well, the lion is their natural enemy, so, when attacked by a lion, they kick it—naturally."

"Very sensible point of view," Ted approved heartily. "Well, you and I aren't lions, therefore Archie won't kick us. Elementary, my dear Watson. Let's go."

Jimmy looked unhappy.

"Twenty-five dollars reward," Ted reminded him, "means we can get that camera."

"Projector," said Jimmy.

"Camera," said Ted. "Come on."

His brother came.

They let themselves cautiously out the back door and, by creeping, managed to get within ten feet of their giraffe before it noticed them. At that point, however, Jimmy fell over the garden hose and into an empty pail, and, the clatter being considerable, Archie withdrew his narrow head from the tree top.

"Shush," said Ted, fiercely.

Jimmy removed himself from the pail with as much dignity as possible. "I couldn't help it. Some silly idiot left that hose across the path."

"You did," said Ted. "Last night."

The giraffe was regarding them in a benign and lofty manner. "The man said to be awfully careful with him," Jimmy said. "He cost thirty-five hundred dollars."

"That thing?" Ted regarded Archie with profound respect. "Well, I'll be hornswoggled! What's he got that I haven't got?"

"More neck," said Jimmy, "and spots with white edgings."

Ted treated this remark with the contempt it deserved. "This is going to be quite simple," he announced suddenly, in a competent manner. "He's perfectly friendly." He stretched out one hand placatingly and began to advance, a step at a time. "Here, Archie, Archie. Nice Archie . . . Ooops!"

Archie gave him one look, shied violently, wheeled and departed around the corner of the house, his sloping body rolling in a ridiculous amble. "Now, look what you've done," said Jimmy. "There goes our projector."

"Camera," said Ted. "Come on. We've got to catch him."

They rushed in pursuit, and, rounding the house, stopped short. "There he is!" Jimmy panted, pointing. "He's stopped. Hey! Ought he to do that?" The giraffe had sighted a yellow crocus in the grass, and it had evidently roused in him a desire for dessert. Accordingly, he had spread his thin forelegs out at an impossible angle and was lowering his head earthwards, in a way that looked extremely perilous.

"He doesn't look safe to me," said Ted. "Besides, for all we know, crocuses aren't good for giraffes. Do they have crocuses in Africa?"

"I don't know," said Jimmy, "but I'll go and get the encyclopedia, while you figure out a way to—"

"Oh, no, you don't," Ted said firmly, grabbing his brother and hauling him back. "I've already figured out a way. How soon do they expect to get here from the zoo?"

"Dunno," Jimmy admitted regretfully. "It's quite a ways, and they may not find our place right off, although I gave 'em directions. Why?"

"If that giraffe leaves," said Ted, "our new camera leaves."

"Projector," said Jimmy.

Ted ignored him. "And the chances are that Archie isn't going to hang around just to oblige us. So *my* idea is to get him into our barn. It's got a good high roof, and—"

"May I ask just one simple little question?" said Jimmy. "*How* are you going to get him into the barn? You can't lead him, you know. He's all neck and legs—there's nothing to hang onto."

Ted said dramatically, "Look at his tail!" Jimmy looked. It was a goodish tail—not beautiful, perhaps, but certainly utilitarian—with a tuft on the end. It would be a most satisfactory tail to hang onto. "Well?" said Ted.

"I can think of two objections," Jimmy said. "One is, do you think you can pull a giraffe around backwards? Because, if so, I'm going to leave the whole thing to you, and you can have the projector all to yourself. I have my life to live."

"It's going to be a camera," Ted said firmly, "and we don't pull him, you goof. We urge him forward gently. The tail is just for emergencies, in case he starts to run."

"Oh," said Jimmy. "Well, the other objection is the location of his tail."

"It's in the usual place, I believe," Ted said stiffly.

"Well, naturally, but the usual place is so awfully near his heels." Jimmy looked mournful and quoted, "They kick with their hind legs and are capable of making a stout resistance."

"So what?" said Ted. "Archie won't attack anything but a lion. You read that yourself from the encyclopedia. We aren't lions, are we?"

There was a short pause. "I see what you mean," said Jimmy. "Are we men or are we lions?" There was another short pause. "Personally, I'm a mouse. You do it, Ted. You're more the executive type. I'll watch."

"You will not," Ted told him. "It's perfectly simple. I'll go in front and urge him on with some grass, and you go behind and hang onto his tail."

"Me?" Jimmy croaked. "Hang onto his tail?"

"Certainly. You just said I was the executive type, didn't you? Well, the executive type always leads. Come on, Jimmy." Ted gave him a shove from behind, and Jimmy staggered mournfully toward Archie's tail, stared at it for a moment, took a deep breath, and grabbed.

Things after that happened very quickly.

Archie's left hind leg kicked out at a fantastic angle and landed a powerful and accurate wallop. Jimmy described a parabola in the air, rolled over twice on the grass, got to his feet, and started running.

Ted joined him.

Archie galloped in enthusiastic pursuit.

His two would-be captors shot up into the branches of the near-est apple tree, and Archie came to a disappointed halt. Jimmy and Ted climbed upward as far as they could and came to rest near an abandoned bird's nest.

They looked at each other.

"Kicks only lions," said Jimmy bitterly. "The executive type—bah!"

"You read the book yourself," Ted accused and looked down thoughtfully at Archie's head, weaving around among the branches. The tree was not tall, and Archie was. After a mo-ment, Ted broke off some juicy-looking leaves and handed them down to Archie, who accepted them courteously. Ted broke off some more.

Jimmy got the idea and began to help. "If we can only keep him here until the zoo men come—"

"I hope the tree lasts out," said Ted. "Sit down, Jimmy. You're rocking the boat."

"Thank you," said his brother with dignity. "I'm more com-fortable standing up."

Ted said, "Oh," with polite sympathy, and Jimmy added, "In case you want to know, being kicked by an even-toed ungulate is the same as being kicked by anything else, only rougher."

"By a what?"

"An even-toed ungulate. That's what that thing down there is. And, personally, I wish he'd go off and ungulate somewhere else."

"Think of the camera," Ted urged.

"I am thinking," said Jimmy, "of the projector." He added broodingly, "So he wouldn't kick me, huh? He wouldn't kick me because I didn't have a mane. Phooey." He then said, "Whoops!" and nearly fell out of the tree.

A large, purposeful-looking truck had just turned into the driveway. "The zoo men!" Ted shouted. "The marines have landed. Jimmy, we're saved." He hesitated, and added, "I wish we weren't up here, though. It doesn't look so good. They might almost think Archie caught *us*."

"If they give that giraffe the reward," said Jimmy, "I shall blow a fuse."

"Hey!" said a voice. A stout man in blue overalls was peering up at them, one arm wound affectionately around Archie's neck. "What you doing up there?"

Jimmy said, "We've caught the giraffe for you," and there was a hearty burst of laughter in response.

"Look who's caught who, will you?" said the stout man. "A nice, tame, little fellow like Archie, too!"

"Tame!" said Ted under his breath, and then addressed the stout man quite coolly. "We couldn't find much for him to eat, and we thought feeding him was the best way to keep him here." He paused impressively. "We're up in this tree—where we can get more leaves."

The stout man was silenced in his turn, and Jimmy and Ted descended with admirable dignity. "Well," the man admitted finally, "that was pretty smart. Yessir, that was real bright. We're much obliged. I'll see you get that reward all right."

Indoors, Jimmy glared at the encyclopedia. "Only lions," he muttered.

"We can get our camera," Ted offered consolingly.

"PROJECTOR!" Jimmy howled.

"M'mmmm," said Ted, "I'll tell you what. We'll compromise. Next time we'll buy a projector. This time we'll buy a camera.

Now run along and get some cookies, there's a pal. All that brain work has made me hungry."

Jimmy gazed upon his brother in mingled awe and fury, said "Compromise!" in a strangled voice, then departed suddenly. He came back, a moment later, both hands full of cookies and a strange glitter in his eyes.

"Ted," he said, "I hate to mention it. But there's a rhinoceros in the back yard."

Ted let out a wild scream and dashed into the kitchen. A moment later, Jimmy heard the back door slam. A gentle smile dawned on his face.

"Ah, well," he murmured, "we can't all be the executive type."

He looked affectionately at the calendar, which still proclaimed unmistakably that it was April Fool's Day, smiled again, and began to eat his cookies. He felt much better.

The Bunny Face

Mildred Jordan

Deb-bee!" called Gertie's high voice from the kitchen door.

"Gertie the Flirtie," Debby and Jerry called their big sister. For Gertie liked the boys. She was pretty, and had yellow curly hair tied with a baby blue ribbon. When Gertie leaned over a steaming washtub, her hair began to tangle like the grapevine, and Gertie pouted. She preferred to dress up and go to the movies. But on the Weissfinger farm, everybody had to work hard before he could have such pleasure.

It was Good Friday, a warm spring day, and the family was astir. This was one of Pop's biggest market days. For the day after tomorrow was Easter; Debby could hardly wait for the egg hunt

19

in the yard on Sunday, when the Easter Rabbit would leave her a nest with yellow and purple grass paper and colored hen's eggs, and a big chocolate egg with "Debby" on it in fancy sugar writing.

Debby was hiding in her regular place in the haymow. She had that curly feeling again. But now it was not because she was going to be naughty, but because she had already done something wrong. She had painted ten of Mom's chicks to take to market and sell today. Nobody knew but Jerry. The chicks, in an old soap carton, were hiding with her in the hay-mow, cheeping noisily. But something was the matter with them. Ever since she had tied strings around their necks and dipped them into the beautiful purple and red and green Easter egg dye she'd found in the tool-house, they all seemed tired, and two of them had died. She was frightened. They were so gay, too, in their new bright-colored coats.

There was a special reason that Debby had stolen the chicks from the hen-house. Last week when she was at market with Mom and Pop in Reading, she had seen a little Easter ornament for sale. It was the most beautiful thing she had seen since a picture of Jesus at Christmas, and she wanted it more than anything in the world. It was a hen's egg, hollowed out, and painted with a rabbit's face. He had long ears of yellow crêpe paper, and a high collar and tie of crêpe paper, too. Debby thought about him all the time. She had coaxed and teased to buy him until her mother threatened to whip her right in the market house; her mother said the Weissfinger family had a better place for twenty-five cents than such trash. But he *wasn't* trash! And Debby had thought of a way to get the Bunny Face. If she colored some chicks, and sold them at market for "two for thirty-nine" like Mrs. Reifsnyder last year, she could buy the Bunny Face and have a lot of money left over for Mom.

"Deb-*bee*," called Gertie again, and this time her voice was a little higher and a little crosser. It was time for Debby to change her dress for market.

Part of Debby wanted to answer Gertie, and get ready for market, and the other part of her was afraid to move. Pop was down in the driveway now, packing into the truck Mom's baked goods, and the jellies and pickled fruits, and all the other things they hoped to sell at market.

Market at Easter time was more exciting than at any other time of the year except Christmas, and Debby would rather go than have a whole pound of licorice to herself. But if Mom found the colored chicks, she would make her stay home, for these were some of the chicks Mom was raising to sell at market later in the spring for fried chicken.

Oh, she almost wished now she hadn't painted the chicks at all. She caressed the little crimson ball in her hand, and he felt limp, like a handful of milkweed. He stopped cheeping so loudly and seemed very tired, and closed his eyes. She was afraid he was going to die too, and he was her favorite. The tears suddenly choked her. She loved these little things so much, it was hard sometimes not to squeeze them to death in her hand.

She was relieved when she heard Jerry steaming along through the barnyard, making a noise like the tractor she could see through her crack in the wall. Jerry knew about her painting the chicks; he would tell her how to get them to market. He wouldn't say she was TOO YOUNG.

"Jerry!" called Debby from the hay. He climbed up the ladder at once, braying like Stubby, the mule.

"I think such another one is going to die yet," whispered Debby, and her voice wobbled like the legs of a new calf.

"Harreyumma," exclaimed Jerry.

Debby and Jerry and all of their family often said queer words like this. Much of the time, the Weissfinger family did not speak English, but a language all mixed up. It was called "Pennsylvania Dutch."

Debby's teacher said that the Pennsylvania Dutch language reminded her of a lamb stew. There was the German, and that was the biggest part, like the meat. Then there was the English, like big hunks of potato. The sprinkling of Welsh and Irish and French words was like the bits of vegetables in the stew—the beans, and carrots and onions.

The reason that the Pennsylvania Dutch talk was like a lamb stew, Debby's teacher said, was because many years ago people left their own countries in Europe and came over to Pennsylvania to live together. Most of the people were German, but some of the people came from other countries, and when they all lived together their language couldn't help but get mixed up.

"Harreyumma!" Jerry said again, "Na come! Pop's got most everything packed in the truck a'ready, and Mom's got her market dress on."

"Jerry, I'm afraid my red one is going to die too yet!"

"Aye-yi-yi, it wonders me you don't kill 'em all, the way you hug and gnoatch 'em and change 'em so from the warm chicken house to the cold barn."

"But what'll Mom say? She'll make me stay home from market."

Jerry scratched his curly red hair. "Ain't, you fixed such a box for them vis holes in?"

Debby pulled the box from under the hay.

"Come, quick na," ordered Jerry, "and I'll hide it behind the potato bag in the truck."

Oh, Jerry was wonderful! He hid them just as he had said he would, and Mom never noticed. She even smiled as Debby came out of the house in her starched red calico, and Pop pulled her pigtails.

Debby began to sing inside of her.

"Easter, Easter, Easter, Easter . . ." she sang.

She couldn't think of anything to rhyme, but "Easter" was enough. It meant so many things she loved: the market, sweet with lilies; the church ringing with organ music—"He is Risen—

He is Risen"; her new straw hat with the roses on it, and the choco-
late-cocoanut Easter egg which would say "DEBBY."

She climbed excitedly into the back of the truck with Jerry, sitting on a carton of Mom's canned peaches. Jerry was whistling
noisily, and winking at her. She began to laugh behind her hand;
Jerry was whistling so Mom couldn't hear the chicks.

Mom and Pop climbed in front, and they waved good-bye to
Gertie and Minnie, and then were chugging down the road.

It was special fun watching the houses and barns and fences
appear and vanish through the opening at the end of the truck,
like scenes in a moving picture. Debby loved to hear the planks
rattle as they went through the old covered bridge, and to see the
sunny river and sky in a quick, thin slice, through a crack of the
dark walls.

The fields and farms stretching off toward the city of Reading
looked much more exciting than they did from the slit in the barn
wall or her bedroom window at home. Most of the Swiss barns
were painted red, and they had overshoots, or slanting roofs off
one side, with stone posts. It was cozy under the overshoot, playing about the tractor when the April showers came. The chickens
often gathered there too, when it rained, to pick clean the "katsa
droke," or cat trough.

Some of the barns had round fancy colored patterns painted
high up on their walls. Grandmom said these were to keep the
witches away. But the minister at the Lutheran church, where the
whole Weissfinger family went every Sunday, said people first put
signs on their barns because they loved Christ, and if you looked
at the pattern closely, it was like a lily. The lily, he said, was a
promise to the early German settlers that they would have a thousand years of peace. Teacher said something still different. She
said the designs were meant to be tulips, and that people used to
believe that wherever Christ walked, the red, red lilies grew.

The farms all looked alike, thought Debby, with their narrow houses made of big stones out of the fields, and a little side porch toward the back, and the grape arbor, the orchard, and the lane of cherry-pie trees, and the outhouse and chicken house and cold-cellar close by. It was the barn that was most beautiful, for the barn was many times bigger than the house, and this was where all the animals lived and all the important things happened.

Pop stopped the truck once at a railroad crossing, and Debby could hear the faint cheep of the chickens under the burlap bag. Surely Mom would hear the chicks this time! She thought again of the Bunny Face. She was closer to it now, and her heart began to beat wildly. What was Mom going to say? And Pop would be angry too, even if the chickens did belong to Mom. Maybe he wouldn't ever talk to Debby again, like Jacob Dreibelbis who lived two farms away, and didn't talk to his wife, Emma. Emma Drei-belbis had once forgotten to take schnitz to market, and Jacob had such a mad on that he still wouldn't talk to her for making him lose money.

But Mom didn't seem to hear the chicks, for Jerry was puffing like the freight train over the hill, and Pop and Mom were laugh-ing at some joke of their own.

Pop drove right to the huge market house, which was in the center of the city of Reading. He parked the truck in the alley, and Debby and Mom and Jerry all helped carry food in to their stall. Every farmer or butcher or Italian fruit man who had a stall, and stood market, was getting the stall ready, arranging food and flowers on his counter. For soon it would be noon and the city people would begin to come with their market baskets.

The market was a lovely place, especially if you were hungry, thought Debby. The building was so large, with its high skylight ceiling, that she could not see the end of it over the heads of the big folks. There were two long, long aisles where soon the people would shuffle up and down with their baskets, stopping to buy food now and then from their favorite farmers.

When would Mom find the chickens, Debby wondered? But she was not too worried, for here she was and Pop couldn't keep her home from market now, although he could use the hickory stick. Jerry had the carton of chicks in his arms, and they were covered with the burlap bag and two boxes of Mom's honey cakes; Jerry was whistling above the crying of the chicks so that his cheeks swelled out like a balloon. There was a lot of noise in the market house, too, and the alley, for everybody was arriving, and the farmers were calling to each other, "Hi, Chake, Hi, Chon—" And there was a scraping of boxes being dragged down the cement floor of the aisles; the angry chatter of live fowl; and the motors of trucks.

Debby skipped. She was glad the Reading people only had petunias and roses in their gardens so that Pop and the other farmers had to come to the city with fruits and vegetables for them to buy. While Mom and Pop and Jerry were busy carrying things, she sneaked away for a moment to the stall where she had seen the Bunny Face. Sure enough, he was still there! And he smiled at her even more invitingly than last week. There was a whole row of Bunny Faces, and some had ears and ties of purple crêpe paper. Their whiskers of ink looked so real, Debby was almost sure she saw them move. And their pink-dotted noses seemed to quiver. The old lady who had the stall smiled at Debby. She was a Mennonite, and wore a plain gray dress and thin net cap.

"Ain't, you're born Weissfinger?" she asked, as she fussed with a box of tiny zinnia plants.

Debby nodded, but was too shy to answer. This was a wonderful stall. There were bouquets of arbutus, and many bunches of herbs for rheumatism and sore fingers and gravy. There were jars of hard candies too, and chocolate rabbits, and a row of Hot Cross Buns, sticky with sugar. Debby's mouth watered. The watercress was still wet from the brook, and there was a mess of early dandelion which Pop loved so to eat with shad. All around the row of

Bunny Faces were little china pots of paper flowers the old lady had made. Under the counter was a big carton of pussy-willows for sale, and many boxes of tiny green plants in black earth, which would be all sold by nighttime to the city people who would transplant them in their gardens.

Debby took one last, long look at the special Bunny Face she liked the best, and hopped away. She was happy. Pretty soon she could hold him in her own hand—just as soon as she had twenty-five cents of her own.

When Debby went back to the Weissfinger stall, Pop was out parking the truck for the day, and Mom was chatting with Sadie Stubblebine in the next stall. Sadie had her whole counter filled with potted plants, and underneath were buckets of cut flowers tied into bouquets. Debby stopped for a moment and drank in the perfume of the lilies, and the hundreds of daffodils, and the knotty arbutus. The splash of color made her start to sing inside again, "Easter, Easter, Easter, Easter . . ." There was nothing in the world more beautiful than the flare of azaleas, the dusky lavender of the tulips, the sharp salmon color of the hothouse sweet peas. They made her dizzy with their sweetness, and the smell of earth that lingered with it. They were more beautiful than anything in the world. . . . Except the Bunny Face, thought Debby, with a stab of pain and desire.

She turned quickly to Jerry, who was balancing a basket of apples on his head and was turning round and round dizzily like the dog when he chased his tail.

"Jerry," she whispered, stopping him and the apples, "what did you do with my chicks?"

"I let them by Aunt Annie's stall," he answered.

Debby glanced at Mom. She was still talking to Sadie Stubblebine, who was laughing and drinking coffee which the Eplinger girl from the restaurant stall had brought around.

"Mom, can I go by Aunt Annie's?" Debby asked anxiously.

Mom stopped for a moment, and pulled Debby's hair-ribbons a little tighter.

"Vy shuah," she said. "Mind you make your manners now. And come back till supper-time."

Debby ran off down the aisle, which was beginning to be crowded. She couldn't see the end of the market house now, but only peoples' waist lines and belts and their market baskets.

Aunt Annie was jolly. She was Debby's favorite aunt. Her eyes twinkled, and she talked fast and mixed her words all up so that she never finished what she was saying. But everybody seemed to know what she meant. She often screwed her face into a knot when she joked, and then people laughed and Aunt Annie laughed, and the world was a wonderful place.

Aunt Annie stood market alone because she had buried Uncle Henry in the family plot in the church graveyard.

"Ach, Himmel, so now you're in the chicken business too yet," she laughed when Debby climbed under the counter. "Look, I laid out the box a'ready and a lady vis a green hat says she comes by again to get some."

Debby's heart fluttered.

"Mom don't know about the chicks," she confessed, and the curly feeling began to wind up inside of her. "Don't retch on me."

"Ain't, you know it makes Bad Luck to begin new work on Good Friday," Aunt Annie said, "like selling chicks?"

Yes, Debby knew that. The men had wanted to come to the farm today and look for water for a new well with a divining rod, but Pop had said "no, you come Mondays. It's bad luck to start anysing on Good Friday."

But nothing could spoil the joy of having something of her own to sell at market. Aunt Annie wrote a sign "2 for 39c" for the chicks, and Debby stood behind them, with her cheeks flushed and her eyes dancing.

Market was a different place than it had ever been when Debby just watched Mom sell corn meal and liver pudding. Now that she was in business, her heart pounded and she watched sharply for customers.

Aunt Annie was too busy to help her. Aunt Annie had a bakery stall, and her hands flew, wrapping up a loaf of home-made rye bread, or a cherry custard tart, or a sunshine cake.

Her tongue and her jokes flew as rapidly as her hands while she made change for her customers.

But the long afternoon passed, and supper-time came, and Debby had not sold one chick. Aunt Annie watched them and gave them water while Debby went to the restaurant stall with Mom and had wiener schnitzel. Debby wasn't hungry. Supposing she didn't sell any chicks at all, and she couldn't buy the Bunny Face?

Mom was in good spirits. "My cup cheese and baked goods are all," she bragged to Mrs. Eplinger, who was dishing out food. "Come, na, Debby, eat once't, Pop and Cherry wait to get their suppah!"

But Debby was only able for half of her dinner. There was a lump in her throat. The lady with the green hat had never come back. . . .

Mom was so busy that she was glad Debby went back to Aunt Annie's stall.

When Debby got there, two more of the little chicks had died, and they seemed smaller now, since their feathers were no longer fluffed up. The tiny crimson chick was breathing hard. Debby held him in her hands to warm him. Tears streamed down her face. In two more hours the market house would be almost empty, and Pop and Mom would be packing up the things that hadn't been sold. The "electric" was turned on now, and the farmers were tired.

"Aye-yi-yi," Aunt Annie was groaning, "such feet! My bunions feel big like an elephant's."

Debby did not answer. Instead, she stole away for a moment

to the Old Lady's stall. There was only one Bunny Face left. She looked at it longingly.

Oh, she *must* sell her chickens. . . .

Crawling back to her corner in Aunt Annie's stall, she waited patiently. Sometimes people stopped and looked at the chicks, and little girls coaxed their parents, but nobody wanted to buy.

"They don't live," some of the fathers said to their little boys.

"They're a nuisance to keep," the mothers said to their little girls.

It was hard to hold the tears back now. Maybe she *was* TOO YOUNG, thought Debby. She didn't know how to sell, like Mom.

Just then a lady hurried past, caught sight of the sign, and came back again. Her arms were filled with bags.

"How many chicks do you have there?" she asked quickly.

"Eight," said Debby, and she thought desperately of the Bunny Face and said, "two for a quarter."

"Eight? Oh, wonderful. They're just what I want for Tim's party tomorrow for favors. I'll take them all."

"Oh!" exclaimed Debby. "Oh!"

Back of the lady was a boy Jerry's size whom she was paying to haul her basket. "Can you carry these, too?" she asked.

She thrust a dollar into Debby's hand, and the boy tucked the carton under his free arm, and they were gone. It happened as fast as a quick wind that blows off your hat.

Debby stared at the dollar in her hand, then raced off to the Old Lady's stall.

"I want the Bunny Face," she panted, and the Egg Rabbit grinned at her gladly. He was tired of being alone.

"Ach, I make it fifteen cents," said the Old Lady, giving Debby change.

The Weissfingers were packing up, and nobody noticed the bag in Debby's hand. Pop was yawning, and Mom was pulling at her corsets. They all worked without talking to get back into the truck the food that remained. Soon they were chugging along the road toward home. Debby and Jerry whispered in the rear of the truck; she had told him about the chicks, and showed him her Bunny Face.

When they turned in their driveway there was a light in the kitchen, and Minnie the Thinnie came to the door, pulling her sweater about her.

"The rats got your baby chicks again," she said to Mom, almost before the truck had stopped.

Debby ran upstairs to bed. She didn't want to hear any more.

When Mom came up later, Debby was saying her prayers in Pennsylvania Dutch, and Debby was very frightened. The Bunny Face was under her sheet.

"Fergeb uns unser shoolda"—

She could see Mom's fat ankles in the doorway, and she prayed hard, "As we forgive those who trespass against us—"

Mom waited until she had said her prayer, and then Mom said, "Deborah Weissfinger—did you color them baby chicks?"

Debby nodded, and trembled.

"Did you sell them by the market?"

Debby nodded again. Mom was shaking all over. Her fat shivered like little ripples of water.

Debby reached under her sheet suddenly and pulled out the Bunny Face and rushed over to Mom, squeezing her about the middle.

"I got you a Easter present," she said, "and here's the money it didn't cost."

She opened the bag and handed her mother the Bunny Face and the eighty-five cents change. The beautiful Bunny Face which she herself wanted more than anything in the world. . . .

Mom tried to hide a smile, but it broke out like the sun from behind a cloud. Then Mom laughed and laughed. Debby began to feel better.

She even laughed a little bit herself.

"Happy Easter, Mom," she cried.

Mom took the Bunny Face, turning it round and round in her fat fingers. Then she handed it back to Debby.

"Dankeschoen," she laughed, putting the money in her pocket, "but you keep the Bunny for me till I make time to play vis it."

Independence Day

∘⟦ *Laura Ingalls Wilder* ⟧∘

Almanzo was eating breakfast before he remembered that this was the Fourth of July. He felt more cheerful.

It was like Sunday morning. After breakfast he scrubbed his face with soft soap till it shone, and he parted his wet hair and combed it sleekly down. He put on his sheep's-gray trousers and his shirt of French calico, and his vest and his short round coat.

Mother had made his new suit in the new style. The coat fastened at the throat with a little flap of the cloth, then the two sides slanted back to show his vest, and they rounded off over his trousers' pockets.

He put on his round straw hat, which Mother had made of braided oat-straws, and he was all dressed up for Independence Day. He felt very fine.

Father's shining horses were hitched to the shining, red-wheeled buggy, and they all drove away in the cool sunshine. All the country had a holiday air. Nobody was working in the fields, and along the road the people in their Sunday clothes were driving to town.

Father's swift horses passed them all. They passed by wagons and carts and buggies. They passed gray horses and black horses and dappled-gray horses. Almanzo waved his hat whenever he sailed past anyone he knew, and he would have been perfectly happy if only he had been driving that swift, beautiful team.

At the church sheds in Malone he helped Father unhitch. Mother and the girls and Royal hurried away. But Almanzo would rather help with the horses than do anything else. He couldn't drive them, but he could tie their halters and buckle on their blankets, and stroke their soft noses and give them hay.

Then he went out with Father and they walked on the crowded sidewalks. All the stores were closed, but ladies and gentlemen were walking up and down and talking. Ruffled little girls carried parasols, and all the boys were dressed up, like Almanzo. Flags were everywhere, and in the Square the band was playing "Yankee Doodle." The fifes tooted and the flutes shrilled and the drums came in with rub-a-dub-dub.

> "Yankee Doodle went to town,
>   Riding on a pony,
> He stuck a feather in his hat,
>   And called it macaroni!"

Even grown-ups had to keep time to it. And there, in the corner of the Square, were the two brass cannons!

The Square was not really square. The railroad made it three-cornered. But everybody called it the Square, anyway. It was fenced, and grass grew there. Benches stood in rows on the grass, and people were filing between the benches and sitting down as they did in church.

Almanzo went with Father to one of the best front seats. All the important men stopped to shake hands with Father. The crowd kept coming till all the seats were full, and still there were people outside the fence.

The band stopped playing, and the minister prayed. Then the band tuned up again and everybody rose. Men and boys took off their hats. The band played, and everybody sang.

"Oh, say, can you see by the dawn's early light,
    What so proudly we hailed at the twilight's last gleaming,
Whose broad stripes and bright stars through the perilous night,
    O'er the ramparts we watched were so gallantly streaming?"

From the top of the flagpole, up against the blue sky, the Stars and Stripes were fluttering. Everybody looked at the American flag, and Almanzo sang with all his might.

Then everyone sat down, and a Congressman stood up on the platform. Slowly and solemnly he read the Declaration of Independence.

"When in the course of human events it becomes necessary for one people . . . to assume among the powers of the earth the separate and equal station. . . . We hold these truths to be self-evident, that all men are created equal. . . ."

Almanzo felt solemn and very proud.

Then two men made long political speeches. One believed in high tariffs, and one believed in free trade. All the grown-ups listened hard, but Almanzo did not understand the speeches very well and he began to be hungry. He was glad when the band played again.

The music was so gay; the bandsmen in their blue and red and their brass buttons tootled merrily, and the fat drummer beat rat-a-tat-tat on the drum. All the flags were fluttering and everybody was happy, because they were free and independent and this was Independence Day. And it was time to eat dinner.

Almanzo helped Father feed the horses while Mother and the girls spread the picnic lunch on the grass in the churchyard. Many others were picnicking there, too, and after he had eaten all he could Almanzo went back to the Square.

There was a lemonade-stand by the hitching-posts. A man sold pink lemonade, a nickel a glass, and a crowd of the town boys were standing around him. Cousin Frank was there. Almanzo had a drink at the town pump, but Frank said he was going to buy lemonade. He had a nickel. He walked up to the stand and bought a glass of the pink lemonade and drank it slowly. He smacked his lips and rubbed his stomach and said:

"Mmmm! Why don't you buy some?"

"Where'd you get the nickel?" Almanzo asked. He had never had a nickel. Father gave him a penny every Sunday to put in the collection-box in church; he had never had any other money.

"My father gave it to me," Frank bragged. "My father gives me a nickel every time I ask him."

"Well, so would my father if I asked him," said Almanzo.

"Well, why don't you ask him?" Frank did not believe that Father would give Almanzo a nickel. Almanzo did not know whether Father would, or not.

"Because I don't want to," he said.

"He wouldn't give you a nickel," Frank said.

"He would, too."

"I dare you to ask him," Frank said. The other boys were listening. Almanzo put his hands in his pockets and said:

"I'd just as lief ask him if I wanted to."

"Yah, you're scared!" Frank jeered. "Double dare! Double dare!"

Father was a little way down the street, talking to Mr. Paddock, the wagon-maker. Almanzo walked slowly toward them. He was faint-hearted, but he had to go. The nearer he got to Father, the

more he dreaded asking for a nickel. He had never before thought
of doing such a thing. He was sure Father would not give it to him.

He waited till Father stopped talking and looked at him.

"What is it, son?" Father asked.

Almanzo was scared. "Father," he said.

"Well, son?"

"Father," Almanzo said, "would you—would you give me—a
nickel?"

He stood there while Father and Mr. Paddock looked at him,
and he wished he could get away. Finally Father asked:

"What for?"

Almanzo looked down at his moccasins and muttered:

"Frank had a nickel. He bought pink lemonade."

"Well," Father said, slowly, "if Frank treated you, it's only right
you should treat him." Father put his hand in his pocket. Then he
stopped and asked:

"Did Frank treat you to lemonade?"

Almanzo wanted so badly to get the nickel that he nodded. Then
he squirmed and said:

"No, Father."

Father looked at him a long time. Then he took out his wallet
and opened it, and slowly he took out a round, big silver half-dollar.
He asked:

"Almanzo, do you know what this is?"

"Half a dollar," Almanzo answered.

"Yes. But do you know what half a dollar is?"

Almanzo didn't know it was anything but half a dollar.

"It's work, son," Father said. "That's what money is; it's hard
work."

Mr. Paddock chuckled. "The boy's too young, Wilder," he said.
"You can't make a youngster understand that."

"Almanzo's smarter than you think," said Father.

Almanzo didn't understand at all. He wished he could get away.

But Mr. Paddock was looking at Father just as Frank looked at Almanzo when he double-dared him, and Father had said Almanzo was smart, so Almanzo tried to look like a smart boy. Father asked:

"You know how to raise potatoes, Almanzo?"

"Yes," Almanzo said.

"Say you have a seed potato in the spring, what do you do with it?"

"You cut it up," Almanzo said.

"Go on, son."

"Then you harrow—first you manure the field, and plow it. Then you harrow, and mark the ground. And plant the potatoes, and plow them, and hoe them. You plow and hoe them twice."

"That's right, son. And then?"

"Then you dig them and put them down cellar."

"Yes. Then you pick them over all winter; you throw out all the little ones and the rotten ones. Come spring, you load them up and haul them here to Malone, and you sell them. And if you get a good price, son, how much do you get to show for all that work? How much do you get for half a bushel of potatoes?"

"Half a dollar," Almanzo said.

"Yes," said Father. "That's what's in this half-dollar, Almanzo. The work that raised half a bushel of potatoes is in it."

Almanzo looked at the round piece of money that Father held up. It looked small, compared with all that work.

"You can have it, Almanzo," Father said. Almanzo could hardly believe his ears. Father gave him the heavy half-dollar.

"It's yours," said Father. "You could buy a sucking pig with it, if you want to. You could raise it, and it would raise a litter of pigs, worth four, five dollars apiece. Or you can trade that half-dollar for lemonade, and drink it up. You do as you want, it's your money."

Almanzo forgot to say thank you. He held the half-dollar a minute, then he put his hand in his pocket and went back to the boys by the lemonade-stand. The man was calling out,

"Step this way, step this way! Ice-cold lemonade, pink lemonade, only five cents a glass! Only half a dime, ice-cold pink lemonade! The twentieth part of a dollar!"

Frank asked Almanzo:

"Where's the nickel?"

"He didn't give me a nickel," said Almanzo, and Frank yelled: "Yah, yah! I told you he wouldn't! I told you so!"

"He gave me half a dollar," said Almanzo.

The boys wouldn't believe it till he showed them. Then they crowded around, waiting for him to spend it. He showed it to them all, and put it back in his pocket.

"I'm going to look around," he said, "and buy me a good little sucking pig."

The band came marching down the street, and they all ran along beside it. The flag was gloriously waving in front, then came the buglers blowing and the fifers tootling and the drummer rattling the drumsticks on the drum. Up the street and down the street went the band, with all the boys following it, and then it stopped in the Square by the brass cannons.

Hundreds of people were there, crowding to watch.

The cannons sat on their haunches, pointing their long barrels upward. The band kept on playing. Two men kept shouting, "Stand back! Stand back!" and other men were pouring black powder into the cannons' muzzles and pushing it down with wads of cloth on long rods.

The iron rods had two handles, and two men pushed and pulled on them, driving the black powder down the brass barrels. Then all the boys ran to pull grass and weeds along the railroad tracks. They carried them by armfuls to the cannons, and the men crowded the weeds into the cannons' muzzles and drove them down with the long rods.

A bonfire was burning by the railroad tracks, and long iron rods were heating in it.

When all the weeds and grass had been packed tight against the powder in the cannons, a man took a little more powder in his hand and carefully filled the two little touchholes in the barrels. Now everybody was shouting,

"Stand back! Stand back!"

Mother took hold of Almanzo's arm and made him come away with her. He told her:

"Aw, Mother, they're only loaded with powder and weeds. I won't get hurt, Mother. I'll be careful, honest." But she made him come away from the cannons.

Two men took the long iron rods from the fire. Everybody was still, watching. Standing as far behind the cannons as they could, the two men stretched out the rods and touched their red-hot tips to the touchholes. A little flame like a candle-flame flickered up from the powder. The little flames stood there burning; nobody breathed. Then—BOOM!

The cannons leaped backward, the air was full of flying grass and weeds. Almanzo ran with all the other boys to feel the warm muzzles of the cannons. Everybody was exclaiming about what a loud noise they had made.

"That's the noise that made the Redcoats run!" Mr. Paddock said to Father.

"Maybe," Father said, tugging his beard. "But it was muskets that won the Revolution. And don't forget it was axes and plows that made this country."

"That's so, come to think of it," Mr. Paddock said.

Independence Day was over. The cannons had been fired, and there was nothing more to do but hitch up the horses and drive home to do the chores.

That night when they were going to the house with the milk, Almanzo asked Father,

"Father, how was it axes and plows that made this country? Didn't we fight England for it?"

"We fought for Independence, son," Father said. "But all the land our forefathers had was a little strip of country, here between the mountains and the ocean. All the way from here west was Indian country, and Spanish and French and English country. It was farmers that took all that country and made it America."

"How?" Almanzo asked.

"Well, son, the Spaniards were soldiers, and high-and-mighty gentlemen that only wanted gold. And the French were fur-traders, wanting to make quick money. And England was busy fighting wars. But we were farmers, son; we wanted the land. It was farmers that went over the mountains, and cleared the land, and settled it, and farmed it, and hung on to their farms.

"This country goes three thousand miles west, now. It goes 'way out beyond Kansas, and beyond the Great American Desert, over mountains bigger than these mountains, and down to the Pacific Ocean. It's the biggest country in the world, and it was farmers who took all that country and made it America, son. Don't you ever forget that."

Thankful

⁂[Mary E. Wilkins Freeman]⁂

Submit Thompson sat on the stone wall; Sarah Adams, an erect, prim little figure, ankle-deep in dry grass, stood beside it, holding Thankful. Thankful was about ten inches long, made of the finest linen, with little rosy cheeks, and a fine little wig of flax. She wore a blue wood frock and a red cloak. Sarah held her close. She even drew a fold of her own blue homespun blanket around her to shield her from the November wind. The sky was low and gray; the wind blew from the northeast, and had the breath of snow in it. Submit on the wall drew her quilted petticoats close down over her feet, and huddled herself into a small space, but her face gleamed keen and resolute out of the depths of a great red hood that belonged to her mother. Her eyes were fixed upon a turkey-

41

32767

KEENE TEACHERS COLLEGE
LIBRARY

gobbler ruffling and bobbing around the back door of the Adams house. The two gambrel-roofed Thompson and Adams houses were built as close together as if the little village of Bridgewater were a city. Acres of land stretched behind them and at the other side, but they stood close to the road, and close to each other. The narrow space between them was divided by a stone wall which was Submit's and Sarah's trysting-place. They met there every day and exchanged confidences. They loved each other like sisters— neither of them had an own sister—but to-day a spirit of rivalry had arisen.

The tough dry blackberry vines on the wall twisted around Submit; she looked, with her circle of red petticoat, like some strange late flower blooming out on the wall. "I know he don't, Sarah Adams," said she.

"Father said he'd weigh twenty pounds," returned Sarah, in a small, weak voice, which still had persistency in it.

"I don't believe he will. Our Thanksgiving turkey is twice as big. You know he is, Sarah Adams."

"No, I don't, Submit Thompson."

"Yes, you do."

Sarah lowered her chin, and shook her head with a decision that was beyond words. She was a thin, delicate-looking little girl, her small blue-clad figure bent before the wind, but there was resolution in her high forehead and her sharp chin.

Submit nodded violently.

Sarah shook her head again. She hugged Thankful, and shook her head, with her eyes still staring defiantly into Submit's hood.

Submit's black eyes in the depths of it were like two sparks. She nodded vehemently; the gesture was not enough for her; she nodded and spoke together. "Sarah Adams," said she, "what will you give me if our turkey is bigger than your turkey?"

"It ain't."

"What will you give me if it is?"

Sarah stared at Submit. "I don't know what you mean, Submit Thompson," said she, with a stately and puzzled air.

"Well, I'll tell you. If your turkey weighs more than ours I'll give you—I'll give you my little workbox with the picture on the top, and if our turkey weighs more than yours you give me— What will you give me, Sarah Adams?"

Sarah hung her flaxen head with a troubled air. "I don't know," said she. "I don't believe I've got anything mother would be willing to have me give away."

"There's Thankful. Your mother wouldn't care if you gave her away."

Sarah started, and hugged Thankful closer. "Yes, my mother would care, too," said she. "Don't you know my Aunt Rose from Boston made her and gave her to me?"

Sarah's beautiful young Aunt Rose from Boston was the special admiration of both the little girls. Submit was ordinarily impressed by her name, but now she took it coolly.

"What if she did?" she returned. "She can make another. It's just made out of a piece of old linen, anyhow. My workbox is real handsome; but you can do just as you are a mind to."

"Do you mean I can have the workbox to keep?" inquired Sarah.

"Course I do, if your turkey's bigger."

Sarah hesitated. "Our turkey is bigger anyhow," she murmured. "Don't you think I ought to ask mother, Submit?" she inquired suddenly.

"No! What for? I don't see anything to ask your mother for. She won't care anything about that rag doll."

"Ain't you going to ask your mother about the workbox?"

"No," replied Submit stoutly. "It's mine; my grandmother gave it to me."

Sarah reflected. "I *know* our turkey is the biggest," she said, looking lovingly at Thankful, as if to justify herself to her. "Well, I don't care," she added, finally.

"Will you?"

"Yes."

"When's yours going to be killed?"

"This afternoon."

"So's ours. Then we'll find out."

Sarah tucked Thankful closer under her shawl. "I know our turkey is biggest," said she. She looked very sober, although her voice was defiant. Just then the great turkey came swinging through the yard. He held up his head proudly and gobbled. His every feather stood out in the wind. He seemed enormous—a perfect giant among turkeys. "*Look* at him!" said Sarah, edging a little closer to the wall; she was rather afraid of him.

"He ain't half so big as ours," returned Submit, stoutly; but her heart sank. The Adams turkey did look very large.

"Submit! Submit!" called a voice from the Thompson house.

Submit slowly got down from the wall. "His feathers are a good deal thicker than ours," she said, defiantly, to Sarah.

"Submit," called the voice, "come right home! I want you to pare apples for the pies. Be quick!"

"Yes, marm," Submit answered back, in a shrill voice; "I'm coming!" Then she went across the yard and into the kitchen door of the Thompson house, like a red robin into a nest. Submit had been taught to obey her mother promptly. Mrs. Thompson was a decided woman.

Sarah looked after Submit, then she gathered Thankful closer, and also went into the house. Her mother, as well as Mrs. Thompson, was preparing for Thanksgiving. The great kitchen was all of a pleasant litter with pie plates and cake pans and mixing bowls, and full of warm, spicy odors. The oven in the chimney was all heated and ready for a batch of apple and pumpkin pies. Mrs. Adams was busy sliding them in; but she stopped to look at Sarah and Thankful. Sarah was her only child.

"Why, what makes you look so sober?" said she.

"Nothing," replied Sarah. She had taken off her blanket, and sat in one of the straight-backed kitchen chairs, holding Thankful.

"You look dreadful sober," said her mother. "Are you tired?"

"No, marm."

"I'm afraid you've got cold standing out there in the wind. Do you feel chilly?"

"No, marm. Mother, how much do you suppose our turkey weighs?"

"I believe father said he'd weigh about twenty pounds. You are sure you don't feel chilly?"

"No, marm. Mother, do you suppose our turkey weighs more than Submit's?"

"How do you suppose I can tell? I ain't set eyes on their turkey lately. If you feel well, you'd better sit up to the table and stone that bowl of raisins. Put your dolly away, and get your apron."

But Sarah stoned raisins with Thankful in her lap, hidden under her apron. She was so full of anxiety that she could not bear to put her away. Suppose the Thompson turkey should be larger, and she should lose Thankful—Thankful that her beautiful Aunt Rose had made for her?

Submit, over in the Thompson house, had sat down at once to her apple paring. She had not gone into the best room to look at the workbox whose possession she had hazarded. It stood in there on the table, made of yellow satiny wood, with a sliding lid ornamented with a beautiful little picture. Submit had a certain pride in it, but her fear of losing it was not equal to her hope of possessing Thankful. Submit had never had a doll, except a few plebeian ones, manufactured secretly out of corncobs, whom it took more imagination than she possessed to admire.

Gradually all emulation over the turkeys was lost in the naughty covetousness of her little friend and neighbor's doll. Submit felt shocked and guilty, but she sat there paring the Baldwin apples, and thinking to herself: "If our turkey is only bigger, if it only is,

then—I shall have Thankful." Her mouth was pursed up and her
eyes snapped. She did not talk at all, but pared very fast.

Her mother looked at her. "If you don't take care, you'll cut your
fingers," said she. "You are in too much of a hurry. I suppose you
want to get out and gossip with Sarah again at the wall, but I can't
let you waste any more time today. There, I told you you would!"

Submit had cut her thumb quite severely. She choked a little
when her mother tied it up, and put on some balm of Gilead, which
made it smart worse.

"Don't cry!" said her mother. "You'll have to bear more than a
cut thumb if you live."

And Submit did not let the tears fall. She came from a brave
race. Her great-grandfather had fought in the Revolution; his
sword and regimentals were packed in the fine carved chest in the
best room. Over the kitchen shelf hung an old musket with which
her great-grandmother, guarding her home and children, had shot
an Indian. In a little closet beside the chimney was an old pewter
dish full of homemade Revolutionary bullets, which Submit and
her brothers had for playthings. A little girl who played with Revolutionary bullets ought not to cry over a cut thumb.

Submit finished paring the apples after her thumb was tied up,
although she was rather awkward about it. Then she pounded
spices in the mortar, and picked over cranberries. Her mother kept
her busy every minute until dinnertime. When Submit's father and
her two brothers, Thomas and Jonas, had come in, she began on
the subject nearest her heart.

"Father," said she, "how much do you think our Thanksgiving
turkey will weigh?"

Mr. Thompson was a deliberate man. He looked at her a minute
before replying. "Seventeen or eighteen pounds," replied he.

"Oh, Father! don't you think he will weigh twenty?" Mr. Thompson shook his head.

"He don't begin to weigh so much as the Adams' turkey," said Jonas. "Their turkey weighs twenty pounds."

"Oh, Thomas! do you think their turkey weighs more than ours?" cried Submit.

Thomas was her elder brother; he had a sober, judicial air like his father. "Their turkey weighs considerable more than ours," said he.

Submit's face fell.

"You are not showing a right spirit," said her mother, severely. "Why should you care if the Adams' turkey does weigh more? I am ashamed of you!"

Submit said no more. She ate her dinner soberly. Afterward she wiped dishes while her mother washed. All the time she was listening. Her father and brothers had gone out; presently she started. "Oh, Mother, they're killing the turkey!" said she.

"Well, don't stop while the dishes are hot, if they are," returned her mother.

Submit wiped obediently, but as soon as the dishes were set away, she stole out in the barn where her father and brothers were picking the turkey.

"Father, when are you going to weigh him?" she asked timidly.

"Not till tonight," said her father.

"Submit!" called her mother.

Submit went in and swept the kitchen floor. It was an hour after that, when her mother was in the south room, getting it ready for her grandparents, who were coming home to Thanksgiving—they had been on a visit to their youngest son—that Submit crept slyly into the pantry. The turkey lay there on the broad shelf before the window. Submit looked at him. She thought he was small. "He was 'most all feathers," she whispered, ruefully. She stood looking disconsolately at the turkey. Suddenly her eyes flashed and a red flush came over her face. It was as if Satan, coming into that godly New England home three days before Thanksgiving, had whispered in her ear.

Presently Submit stole softly back into the kitchen, set a chair before the chimney cupboard, climbed up, and got the pewter dish full of Revolutionary bullets. Then she stole back to the pantry and emptied the bullets into the turkey's crop. Then she got a needle and thread from her mother's basket, sewed up the crop carefully, and set the empty dish back in the cupboard. She had just stepped down out of the chair when her brother Jonas came in.

"Submit," said he, "let's have one game of odd or even with the bullets."

"I am too busy," said Submit. "I've got to spin my stint."

"Just one game. Mother won't care."

"No; I can't."

Submit flew to her spinning wheel in the corner. Jonas, still remonstrating, strolled into the pantry.

"I don't believe Mother wants you in there," Submit said anxiously.

"See here, Submit," Jonas called out in an eager voice, "I'll get the steelyards, and we'll weigh the turkey. We can do it as well as anybody."

Submit left her spinning wheel. She was quite pale with trepidation when Jonas and she adjusted the turkey in the steelyards. What if those bullets should rattle out? But they did not.

"He weighs twenty pounds and a quarter," announced Jonas, with a gasp, after peering anxiously at the figures. "He's the biggest turkey that was ever raised in these parts."

Jonas exulted a great deal, but Submit did not say much. As soon as Jonas had laid the turkey back on the shelf and gone out, she watched her chance and removed the bullets, replacing them in the pewter dish.

When Mr. Thompson and Thomas came home at twilight there was a deal of talk over the turkey.

"The Adams' turkey doesn't weigh but nineteen pounds," Jonas announced. "Sarah was out there when they weighed him, and she 'most cried."

"I think Sarah and Submit and all of you are very foolish about it," said Mrs. Thompson severely. "What difference does it make if one weighs a pound or two more than the other, if there is enough to go round?"

"Submit looks as if she was sorry ours weighed the most now," said Jonas.

"My thumb aches," said Submit.

"Go and get the balm of Gilead bottle, and put some more on," ordered her mother.

That night when she went to bed she could not say her prayers. When she woke in the morning it was with a strange, terrified feeling, as if she had climbed a wall into some unknown dreadful land. She wondered if Sarah would bring Thankful over; she dreaded to see her coming, but she did not come. Submit herself did not stir out of the house all that day or the next, and Sarah did not bring Thankful until next morning.

They were all out in the kitchen about an hour before dinner. Grandfather Thompson sat in his old armchair at one corner of the fireplace, Grandmother Thompson was knitting, and Jonas and Submit were cracking butternuts. Submit was a little happier this morning. She thought Sarah would never bring Thankful, and so she had not done so much harm by cheating in the weight of the turkey.

There was a tug at the latch of the kitchen door; it was pushed open slowly and painfully, and Sarah entered with Thankful in her arms. She said not a word to anybody, but her little face was full of woe. She went straight to Submit, and laid Thankful in her lap; then she turned and fled with a great sob. The door slammed after her. All the Thompsons stopped and looked at Submit.

"Submit, what does this mean?" her father asked.

Submit looked at him, trembling.

"Speak," said he.

"Submit, mind your father," said Mrs. Thompson.

"What did she bring you the doll baby for?" asked Grandmother Thompson.

"Sarah—was going to give me Thankful if—our turkey weighed most, and I was going to—give her my—work-box if hers weighed most," said Submit jerkily. Her lips felt stiff.

Her father looked very sober and stern. He turned to his father. When Grandfather Thompson was at home, every one deferred to him. Even at eighty he was the recognized head of the house. He was a wonderful old man, tall and soldierly, and full of a grave dignity. He looked at Submit, and she shrank.

"Do you know," said he, "that you have been conducting yourself like unto the brawlers in the taverns and ale-houses?"

"Yes, sir," murmured Submit, although she did not know what he meant.

"No godly maid who heeds her elders will take part in any such foolish and sinful wager," her grandfather continued.

Submit arose, hugging Thankful convulsively. She glanced wildly at her great-grandmother's musket over the shelf. The same spirit that had aimed it at the Indian possessed her, and she spoke out quite clearly: "Our turkey didn't weigh the most," said she. "I put the Revolutionary bullets in his crop."

There was silence. Submit's heart beat so hard that Thankful quivered.

"Go upstairs to your chamber, Submit," said her mother, "and you need not come down to dinner. Jonas, take that doll and carry it over to the Adams' house."

Submit crept miserably out of the room, and Jonas carried Thankful across the yard to Sarah.

Submit crouched beside her little square window set with tiny panes of glass, and watched him. She did not cry. She was very miserable, but confession had awakened a salutary smart in her soul, like the balm of Gilead on her cut thumb. She was not so unhappy as she had been. She wondered if her father would whip her, and she made up her mind not to cry if he did.

After Jonas came back she still crouched at the window. Exactly opposite in the Adams' house was another little square window, and that lighted Sarah's chamber. All of a sudden Sarah's face appeared there. The two little girls stared pitifully at each other. Presently Sarah raised her window, and put a stick under it; then Submit did the same. They put their faces out, and looked at each other a minute before speaking. Sarah's face was streaming with tears.

"What you crying for?" called Submit softly.

"Father sent me up here 'cause it is sinful to—make bets, and Aunt Rose has come, and I can't have any—Thanksgiving dinner," wailed Sarah.

"I'm wickeder than you," said Submit. "I put the Revolutionary bullets in the turkey to make it weigh more than yours. Yours weighed the most. If mother thinks it's right, I'll give you the work-box."

"I don't—want it," sobbed Sarah. "I'm dreadful sorry you've got to stay up there, and can't have any dinner, Submit."

Answering tears sprang to Submit's eyes. "I'm dreadful sorry you've got to stay up there, and can't have any dinner," she sobbed back.

There was a touch on her shoulder. She looked around and there stood the grandmother. She was trying to look severe, but she was beaming kindly on her. Her fat, fair old face was as gentle as the mercy that tempers justice; her horn spectacles and her knitting needles and the gold beads on her neck all shone in the sunlight.

"You had better come downstairs, child," said she. "Dinner's 'most ready, and mebbe you can help your mother. Your father isn't going to whip you this time, because you told the truth about it, but you mustn't ever do such a dreadful wicked thing again."

"No, I won't," sobbed Submit. She looked across, and there beside Sarah's face in the window was another beautiful smiling one. It had pink cheeks and sweet black eyes and black curls, among which stood a high tortoise-shell comb.

"Oh, Submit!" Sarah called out, joyfully, "Aunt Rose says I can go down to dinner!"

"Grandmother says I can!" called back Submit.

The beautiful smiling face opposite leaned close to Sarah's for a minute.

"Oh, Submit!" cried Sarah, "Aunt Rose says she will make you a doll baby like Thankful, if your mother's willing!"

"I guess she'll be willing if she's a good girl," called Grandmother Thompson.

Submit looked across a second in speechless radiance. Then the faces vanished from the two little windows, and Submit and Sarah went down to their Thanksgiving dinners.

Master of all Masters

ᵒ[*Joseph Jacobs*]ᵒ

A girl once went to the fair to hire herself for servant. At last a funny-looking old gentleman engaged her, and took her home to his house. When she got there he told her that he had something to teach her, for that in his house he had his own names for things.

He said to her: "What will you call me?"

"Master or mister, or whatever you please, sir," says she.

He said: "You must call me 'master of all masters.' And what would you call this?" pointing to his bed.

"Bed or couch, or whatever you please, sir."

"No, that's my 'barnacle.' And what do you call these?" said he, pointing to his pantaloons.

"Breeches or trousers, or whatever you please, sir."

"You must call them 'squibs and crackers.' And what would you call her?" pointing to the cat.

"Cat or kit, or whatever you please, sir."

"You must call her 'white-faced simminy.' And this now," showing the fire, "what would you call this?"

"Fire or flame, or whatever you please, sir."

"You must call it 'hot cockalorum,' and what this?" he went on, pointing to the water.

"Water or wet, or whatever you please, sir."

"No, 'pondalorum' is its name. And what do you call all this?" asked he, as he pointed to the house.

"House or cottage, or whatever you please, sir."

"You must call it 'high topper mountain.'"

That very night the servant woke her master up in a fright and said: "Master of all masters, get out of your barnacle and put on your squibs and crackers. For white-faced simminy has got a spark of hot cockalorum on its tail, and unless you get some pondalorum high topper mountain will be all on hot cockalorum." . . . That's all.

The Peterkins Celebrate the Fourth of July

ᵒᵷ[*Lucretia Hale*]ᵒᵷ

The day began early.

A compact had been made with the little boys the evening before.

They were to be allowed to usher in the glorious day by the blowing of horns exactly at sunrise. But they were to blow them for precisely five minutes only, and no sound of the horns should be heard afterward till the family were downstairs.

It was thought that a peace might thus be bought by a short, though crowded, period of noise.

55

The morning came. Even before the morning, at half-past three o'clock, a terrible blast of the horns aroused the whole family.

Mrs. Peterkin clasped her hands to her head and exclaimed: "I am thankful the lady from Philadelphia is not here!" For she had been invited to stay a week, but had declined to come before the Fourth of July, as she was not well, and her doctor had prescribed quiet.

And the number of the horns was most remarkable! It was as though every cow in the place had arisen and was blowing through both her own horns!

"How many little boys are there? How many have we?" exclaimed Mr. Peterkin, going over their names one by one mechanically, thinking he would do it, as he might count imaginary sheep jumping over a fence, to put himself to sleep. Alas! the counting could not put him to sleep now, in such a din.

And how unexpectedly long the five minutes seemed! Elizabeth Eliza was to take out her watch and give the signal for the end of the five minutes, and the ceasing of the horns. Why did not the signal come? Why did not Elizabeth Eliza stop them?

And certainly it was long before sunrise; there was no dawn to be seen!

"We will not try this plan again," said Mrs. Peterkin.

"If we live to another Fourth," added Mr. Peterkin, hastening to the door to inquire into the state of affairs.

Alas! Amanda, by mistake, had waked up the little boys an hour too early. And by another mistake the little boys had invited three or four of their friends to spend the night with them. Mrs. Peterkin had given them permission to have the boys for the whole day, and they understood the day as beginning when they went to bed the night before. This accounted for the number of horns.

It would have been impossible to hear any explanation; but the five minutes were over, and the horns had ceased, and there remained only the noise of a singular leaping of feet, explained perhaps by a possible pillow-fight, that kept the family below partially awake until the bells and cannon made known the dawning of the glorious day—the sunrise, or "the rising of the sons," as Mr. Peterkin jocosely called it when they heard the little boys and their friends clattering down the stairs to begin the outside festivities.

They were bound first for the swamp, for Elizabeth Eliza, at the suggestion of the lady from Philadelphia, had advised them to hang some flags around the pillars of the piazza. Now the little boys knew of a place in the swamp where they had been in the habit of digging for "flag-root," and where they might find plenty of flag flowers. They did bring away all they could, but they were a little out of bloom. The boys were in the midst of nailing up all they had on the pillars of the piazza, when the procession of the Antiques and Horribles passed along. As the procession saw the festive arrangements on the piazza, and the crowd of boys, who cheered them loudly, it stopped to salute the house with some especial strains of greeting.

Poor Mrs. Peterkin! They were directly under her windows! In a few moments of quiet, during the boys' absence from the house on their visit to the swamp, she had been trying to find out whether she had a sick headache, or whether it was all the noise, and she was just deciding it was the sick headache, but was falling into a light slumber, when the fresh noise outside began.

There were the imitations of the crowing of cocks, and braying of donkeys, and the sound of horns, encored and increased by the cheers of the boys. Then began the torpedoes, and the Antiques and Horribles had Chinese crackers also.

And, in despair of sleep, the family came down to breakfast.

Mrs. Peterkin had always been much afraid of fireworks, and had never allowed the boys to bring gunpowder into the house. She was even afraid of torpedoes; they looked so much like sugar-plums she was sure some of the children would swallow them, and explode before anybody knew it.

She was very timid about other things. She was not sure even about peanuts. Everybody exclaimed over this: "Surely there was no danger in peanuts!" But Mrs. Peterkin declared she had been very much alarmed at the Centennial Exhibition, and in the crowded corners of the streets in Boston, at the peanut stands, where they had machines to roast the peanuts. She did not think it was safe. They might go off any time, in the midst of a crowd of people, too!

Mr. Peterkin thought there actually was no danger, and he should be sorry to give up the peanut. He thought it an American institution, something really belonging to the Fourth of July. He even confessed to a quiet pleasure in crushing the empty shells with his feet on the sidewalks as he went along the streets.

Agamemnon thought it a simple joy.

In consideration, however, of the fact that they had had no real celebration of the Fourth the last year, Mrs. Peterkin had consented to give over the day, this year, to the amusement of the family as a Centennial celebration. She would prepare herself for a terrible noise—only she did not want any gunpowder brought into the house.

The little boys had begun by firing some torpedoes a few days beforehand, that their mother might be used to the sound, and had selected their horns some weeks before.

Solomon John had been very busy in inventing some fireworks. As Mrs. Peterkin objected to the use of gunpowder, he found out from the dictionary what the different parts of gunpowder are—saltpetre, charcoal, and sulphur. Charcoal, he discovered, they had in the wood-house; saltpetre they would find in the cellar, in the beef barrel; and sulphur they could buy at the apothecary's. He explained to his mother that these materials had never yet exploded in the house, and she was quieted.

Agamemnon, meanwhile, remembered a recipe he had read somewhere for making a "fulminating paste" of iron-filings and powder of brimstone. He had written it down on a piece of paper in his pocketbook. But the iron filings must be finely powdered. This they began upon a day or two before, and the very afternoon before laid out some of the paste on the piazza.

Pinwheels and rockets were contributed by Mr. Peterkin for the evening. According to a program drawn up by Agamemnon and Solomon John, the reading of the Declaration of Independence was to take place in the morning, on the piazza, under the flags.

The Bromwicks brought over their flag to hang over the door.

"That is what the lady from Philadelphia meant," explained Elizabeth Eliza.

"She said the flags of our country," said the little boys. "We thought she meant 'in the country.'"

Quite a company assembled; but it seemed nobody had a copy of the Declaration of Independence.

Elizabeth Eliza said she could say one line, if they each could add as much. But it proved they all knew the same line that she did, as they began:

"When, in the course of—when, in the course of—when, in the course of human—when in the course of human events—when, in the course of human events, it becomes—when, in the course of human events, it becomes necessary—when in the course of human events, it becomes necessary for one people"—

They could not get any farther. Some of the party decided that "one people" was a good place to stop, and the little boys sent off some fresh torpedoes in honor of the people. But Mr. Peterkin was not satisfied. He invited the assembled party to stay until sunset, and meanwhile he would find a copy, and torpedoes were to be saved to be fired off at the close of every sentence.

And now the noon bells rang and the noon bells ceased.

Mrs. Peterkin wanted to ask every body to dinner. She should have some cold beef. She had let Amanda go, because it was the

Fourth, and everybody ought to be free that one day; so she could not have much of a dinner. But when she went to cut her beef she found Solomon had taken it to soak, on account of the saltpetre, for the fireworks!

Well, they had a pig; so she took a ham, and the boys had bought tamarinds and buns and a cocoanut. So the company stayed on, and when the Antiques and Horribles passed again they were treated to peanuts and lemonade.

They sung patriotic songs, they told stories, they fired torpedoes, they frightened the cats with them. It was a warm afternoon; the red poppies were out wide, and the hot sun poured down on the alleyways in the garden. There was a seething sound of a hot day in the buzzing of insects, in the steaming heat that came up from the ground. Some neighboring boys were firing a toy cannon. Every time it went off Mrs. Peterkin started, and looked to see if one of the little boys was gone. Mr. Peterkin had set out to find a copy of the "Declaration." Agamemnon had disappeared. She had not a moment to decide about her headache. She asked Ann Maria if she were not anxious about the fireworks, and if rockets were not dangerous. They went up, but you were never sure where they came down.

And then came a fresh tumult! All the fire engines in town rushed toward them, clanging with bells, men and boys yelling! They were out for a practice, and for a Fourth-of-July show.

Mrs. Peterkin thought the house was on fire, and so did some of the guests. There was great rushing hither and thither. Some thought they would better go home; some thought they would better stay. Mrs. Peterkin hastened into the house to save herself, or see what she could save. Elizabeth Eliza followed her, first proceeding to collect all the pokers and tongs she could find, because they could be thrown out of the window without breaking. She had read of people who had flung looking glasses out of the window by mistake, in the excitement of the house being on fire, and had carried the pokers and tongs carefully into the garden. There was nothing like being prepared. She had always determined to do the reverse. So with calmness she told Solomon John to take down the looking glasses. But she met with a difficulty—there were no pokers and tongs, as they did not use them. They had no open fires; Mrs. Peterkin had been afraid of them. So Elizabeth Eliza took all the pots and kettles up to the upper windows, ready to be thrown out.

But where was Mrs. Peterkin? Solomon John found she had fled to the attic in terror. He persuaded her to come down, assuring her it was the most unsafe place; but she insisted upon stopping to collect some bags of old pieces, that nobody would think of saving from the general wreck, she said, unless she did. Alas! This was the result of fireworks on Fourth of July! As they came downstairs they heard the voices of all the company declaring there was no fire; the danger was past. It was long before Mrs. Peterkin could believe it. They told her the fire company was only out for show, and to celebrate the Fourth of July. She thought it already too much celebrated.

Elizabeth Eliza's kettles and pans had come down through the windows with a crash, that had only added to the festivities, the little boys thought.

Mr. Peterkin had been roaming about all this time in search of a copy of the Declaration of Independence. The public library was shut, and he had to go from house to house; but now, as the sunset bells and cannon began, he returned with a copy and read it, to the pealing of the bells and sounding of the cannon. Torpedoes and crackers were fired at every pause. Some sweet-marjoram pots, tin cans filled with crackers which were lighted, went off with great explosions.

At the most exciting moment, near the close of the reading, Agamemnon, with an expression of terror, pulled Solomon John aside.

"I have suddenly remembered where I read about the 'fulminating paste' we made. It was in the preface to 'Woodstock,' and I have been round to borrow the book, to read the directions over again, because I was afraid about the 'paste' going off. READ THIS QUICKLY! and tell me, *Where is the fulminating paste?*"

Solomon John was busy winding some covers of paper over a little parcel. It contained chlorate of potash and sulphur mixed. A friend had told him of the composition. The more thicknesses of paper you put round it the louder it would go off. You must pound it with a hammer. Solomon John felt it must be perfectly safe, as his mother had taken potash for a medicine.

He still held the parcel as he read from Agamemnon's book: "This paste, when it has lain together about twenty-six hours, will *of itself* take fire, and burn all the sulphur away with a blue flame and a bad smell."

"Where is the paste?" repeated Solomon John, in terror.

"We made it just twenty-six hours ago," said Agamemnon.

"We put it on the piazza," explained Solomon John, rapidly recalling the facts, "and it is in front of our mother's feet!"

He hastened to snatch the paste away before it should take fire, flinging aside the packet in his hurry. Agamemnon, jumping upon the piazza at the same moment, trod upon the paper parcel, which exploded at once with the shock, and he fell to the ground, while at the same moment the paste "fulminated" into a blue flame directly in front of Mrs. Peterkin!

It was a moment of great confusion. There were cries and screams. The bells were still ringing, the cannon firing, and Mr. Peterkin had just reached the closing words: "Our lives, our fortunes, and our sacred honor."

"We are all blown up, as I feared we should be," Mrs. Peterkin at length ventured to say, finding herself in a lilac bush by the side of the piazza. She scarcely dared to open her eyes to see the scattered limbs about her.

It was so with all. Even Ann Maria Bromwick clutched a pillar of the piazza, with closed eyes.

At length Mr. Peterkin said, calmly, "Is anybody killed?"

There was no reply. Nobody could tell whether it was because everybody was killed, or because they were too wounded to answer. It was a great while before Mrs. Peterkin ventured to move.

But the little boys soon shouted with joy, and cheered the success of Solomon John's fireworks, and hoped he had some more. One of them had his face blackened by an unexpected cracker, and Elizabeth Eliza's muslin dress was burned here and there. But no one was hurt; no one had lost any limbs, though Mrs. Peterkin was sure she had seen some flying in the air. Nobody could understand how, as she had kept her eyes firmly shut.

No greater accident had occurred than the singeing of the tip of Solomon John's nose. But there was an unpleasant and terrible odor from the "fulminating paste."

Mrs. Peterkin was extricated from the lilac bush. No one knew how she got there. Indeed, the thundering noise had stunned everybody. It had roused the neighborhood even more than before. Answering explosions came on every side, and, though the sunset light had not faded away, the little boys hastened to send off rockets under cover of the confusion. Solomon John's other fireworks would not go. But all felt he had done enough.

Mrs. Peterkin retreated into the parlor, deciding she really did have a headache. At times she had to come out when a rocket went off, to se if it was one of the little boys. She was exhausted by the adventures of the day, and almost thought it could not have been worse if the boys had been allowed gunpowder. The distracted lady was thankful there was likely to be but one Centennial Fourth in her lifetime, and declared she should never more keep anything in the house as dangerous as saltpetred beef, and she should never venture to take another spoonful of potash.

The Magic Ball

°⟦ *Charles Finger* ⟧°

(A TALE OF THE CHUPUT COUNTRY)

A cold-eyed witch lived in the Cordilleras and when the first
snow commenced to fall she was always full of glee, standing on
a rock, screaming like a wind-gale and rubbing her hands. For it
pleased her to see the winter moon, the green country blotted out,
the valleys white, the trees snow-laden, and the waters ice-bound
and black. Winter was her hunting time and her eating time, and
in the summer she slept. So she was full of a kind of savage joy
when there were leaden clouds and drifting gales, and she waited
and watched, waited and watched, ever ready to spring upon frost-
stiffened creatures, that went wandering down to the warmer
lowlands.

This witch was a wrinkled creature, hard of eye, thin-lipped, with hands that looked like roots of trees, and so tough was her skin that knife could not cut nor arrow pierce it. In the country that swept down to the sea she was greatly feared, and hated, too. The hate came because by some strange magic she was able to draw children to her one by one, and how she did it no man knew. But the truth is that she had a magic ball, a ball bright and shining and of many colors, and this she left in places where children played, but never where man or woman could see it.

One day, near the lake called Oretta, a brother and sister were at play and saw the magic ball at the foot of a little hill. Pleased with its brightness and beauty Natalia ran to it, intending to pick it up and take it home, but, to her surprise, as she drew near to it the ball rolled away; then, a little way off, came to rest again. Again she ran to it and almost had her hand on it when it escaped, exactly as a piece of thistle-down does, just as she was about to grasp it. So she followed it, always seeming to be on the point of catching it but never doing so, and as she ran her brother Luis followed, careful lest she should come to harm. The strange part of it was that every time the ball stopped it rested close to some berry bush or by the edge of a crystal-clear spring, so that she, like all who were thus led away, always found at the moment of resting something to eat or to drink or to refresh herself. Nor, strangely enough, did she tire, but because of the magic went skipping and running and jumping just as long as she followed the ball. Nor did any one under the spell of that magic note the passing of time, for days were like hours and a night like the shadow of a swiftly flying cloud.

At last, chasing the ball, Natalia and Luis came to a place in the valley where the Rio Chico runs between great hills, and it was dark and gloomy and swept by heavy gray clouds. The land was strewn with mighty broken rocks and here and there were patches of snow, and soon great snowflakes appeared in the air. Then boy and girl were terrorstruck, for they knew with all the wandering and twisting and turning they had lost their way. But the ball still rolled on, though slower now, and the children followed. But the air grew keener and colder and the sun weaker, so that they were very glad indeed when they came to a black rock where, at last, the ball stopped.

Natalia picked it up, and for a moment gazed at its beauty, but for a moment only. For no sooner had she gazed at it and opened her lips to speak than it vanished as a soap bubble does, at which her grief was great. Luis tried to cheer her and finding that her hands were icy cold led her to the north side of the rock where it was warmer, and there he found a niche like a lap between two great arms, and in the moss grown cranny Natalia coiled herself up and was asleep in a minute. As for Luis, knowing that as soon as his sister had rested they must set out about finding a way home, he sat down intending to watch. But not very long did he keep his eyes open, for he was weary and sad at heart. He tried hard to keep awake, even holding his eyelids open with his fingers, and he stared hard at a sunlit hilltop across the valley, but even that seemed to make him sleepy. Then, too, there were slowly nodding pine trees and the whispering of leaves, coming in a faint murmur from the mountainside. So, soon, Luis slept.

Natalia, being out of the blustering wind, was very comfortable in the little niche between the great stone arms, and she dreamed that she was at home. Her mother, she thought, was combing her hair and singing as she did so. So she forgot her hunger and weariness, and in her dreamland knew nothing of the bare black rocks and snow-patched hills. Instead, she seemed to be at home where the warm firelight danced on the walls and lighted her father's brown face to a lively red as he mended his horse gear. She saw her brother, too, with his jet-black hair and cherry-red lips. But her mother, she thought, grew rough and careless and pulled her hair, so that she gave a little cry of pain and awoke. Then in a flash she knew where she was and was chilled to the bone with the piercing wind that swept down from the mountain top. Worse still, in front of her stood the old witch of the hills, pointing, pointing, pointing with knotty forefinger, and there were nails on her hands and feet that looked like claws.

Natalia tried to rise, but could not, and her heart was like stone when she found what had happened. It was this: while she slept, the witch had stroked and combed her hair, and meanwhile wrought magic, so that the girl's hair was grown into the rock so very close that she could not as much as turn her head. All that she could do was to stretch forth her arms, and when she saw Luis a little way off she called to him most piteously. But good Luis made no move. Instead, he stood with arms wide apart like one who feels a wall in the dark, moving his hands this way and that. Then Natalia wept, not understanding and little knowing that the witch had bound Luis with a spell, so that there seemed to be an invisible wall around the rock through which he could not pass, try as he would. But he heard the witch singing in her high and cracked voice, and this is what she sang:

> "Valley all pebble-sown,
>   Valley where wild winds moan!
>   Come, mortals, come.
>
> "Valley so cool and white,
>   Valley of winter night,
>   Come, children, come.
>
> "Straight like a shaft to mark,
>   Come they to cold and dark,
>   Children of men!"

Then she ceased and stood with her root-like finger upraised, and from near by came the voice of a great white owl, which took up the song, saying:

"Things of the dark and things without name,
Save us from light and the torch's red flame."

Now all this was by starlight, but the moment the owl had ceased, from over the hill came a glint of light as the pale moon rose, and with a sound like a thunderclap the witch melted into the great rock and the owl flapped away heavily.

"Brother," whispered the girl, "you heard what the owl said?"

"Yes, sister, I heard," he answered.

"Brother, come to me. I am afraid," said Natalia, and commenced to cry a little.

"Sister," he said, "I try but I cannot. There is something through which I cannot pass. I can see but I cannot press through."

"Can you not climb over, dear Luis?" asked Natalia.

"No, Natalia. I have reached high as I can, but the wall that I cannot see goes up and up."

"Is there no way to get in on the other side of the rock, dear, dear Luis? I am very cold and afraid, being here alone."

"Sister, I have walked around. I have felt high and low. But it is always the same. I cannot get through, I cannot climb over, I cannot crawl under. But I shall stay here with you, so fear not."

At that Natalia put her hands to her face and wept a little, but very quietly, and it pained Luis to see the tears roll down her cheeks and turn to little ice pearls as they fell. After a while Natalia spoke again, but through sobs.

"Brother mine, you heard what the owl said?"

"Yes, sister."

"Does it mean nothing to you?" she asked.

"Nothing," he replied.

"But listen," said Natalia. "These were the words: 'Save us from light and the torch's red flame.' "

"I heard that, Natalia. What does it mean?"

"It means, brother, that the things in this horrible valley fear fire.

So go, brother. Leave me a while but find fire, coming back with it swiftly. There will be sickening loneliness, so haste, haste."

Hearing that, Luis was sad, for he was in no mood to leave his sister in that plight. Still she urged him, saying: "Speed, brother, speed."

Even then he hesitated, until with a great swoop there passed over the rock a condor wheeling low, and it said as it passed: "Fire will conquer frosted death."

"You hear, brother," said Natalia. "So speed and find fire and return before night."

Then Luis stayed no longer, but waved his sister a farewell and set off down the valley, following the condor that hovered in the air, now darting away and now returning. So Luis knew that the great bird led him, and he ran, presently finding the river and following it until he reached the great vega where the waters met.

At the meeting of the waters he came to a house, a poor thing made of earth and stones snuggled in a warm fold of the hills. No one was about there, but as the condor flew high and, circling in the air, became a small speck, Luis knew that it would be well to stay a while and see what might befall. Pushing open the door he saw by the ashes in the fireplace that someone lived there, for there were red embers well covered to keep the fire alive. So seeing that the owner of the house would return soon he made himself free of the place, which was the way of that country, and brought fresh water from the spring. Then he gathered wood and piled it neatly by the fireside. Next he blew upon the embers and added twigs and sticks until a bright fire glowed, after which he took the broom of twigs and swept the earth floor clean.

How the man of the house came into the room Luis never knew, but there he was, sitting by the fire on a stool. He looked at things but said nothing to Luis, only nodding his head. Then he brought bread and yerba and offered some to Luis. After they had eaten the old man spoke, and this is what he said:

"Wicked is the white witch, and there is but one way to defeat her. What, lad, is the manner of her defeat? Tell me that."

Then Luis, remembering what the condor had said, repeated the words: " 'Fire will conquer frosted death.' "

"True," said the man slowly, nodding his head. "And your sister is there. Now here comes our friend the condor, who sees far and knows much."

> "Now with cold grows faint her breath,
> Fire will conquer frosted death."

Having said that the great bird wheeled up sharply.

But no sooner was it out of sight than a turkey came running and stood a moment, gobbling. To it the old man gave a lighted brand, repeating the words the condor had spoken.

Off sped the turkey with the blazing stick, running through marsh and swamp in a straight line, and Luis and the old man watched. Soon the bird came to a shallow lagoon, yet made no halt. Straight through the water it sped, and so swiftly that the spray dashed up on either side. High the turkey held the stick, but not high enough, for the splashing water quenched the fire, and seeing that, the bird returned, dropping the blackened stick at the old man's feet.

"Give me another, for the maiden is quivering cold," said the turkey. "This time I will run round the lake."

"No. No." answered the man. "You must know that when the water spirit kisses the fire king, the fire king dies. So, that you may remember, from now and for ever you will carry on your feathers the marks of rippling water."

Down again swooped the condor and a little behind him came a goose, flying heavily. As before, the condor cried:

> "Now with cold grows faint her breath,
> Fire will conquer frosted death,"

then flew away again toward the witch mountain.

To the goose the old man gave a blazing stick and at once the brave bird set off, flying straight in the direction the condor had taken. Over vega and over lagoon she went, pausing only at a snow-clad hilltop, because the stick had burned closer to her beak. So she dropped it in the snow to get a better hold, and when she picked it up again there was but a charred thing. Sad enough the goose returned to the house, bearing the blackened stick, and begged to be given another chance.

"No. No," said the old man. "The silver snow queen's kiss is death to the fire king. That is something you must remember. From now on and for ever you must carry feathers of gray like the ashes. But here comes the condor and we must hear his message."

Sadly then the goose went away, her feathers ash gray, and the condor wheeled low again, calling:

> "Fainter grows the maiden's breath,
> Night must bring the frosted death,"

and having said, like an arrow he shot off.

No sooner had he gone than the long-legged, long-billed flamingo dropped to the ground.

"Your beak is long," said the old man, "but fly swiftly, for the stick is short."

The flamingo took the burning stick by the end and made straight for the mountain, racing with all possible speed. As for Luis, he made up his mind to tarry no longer and set off, running like a deer. But an ostrich, seeing him, spread her wings like sails and ran by his side. On her back Luis placed his hand, and with that help sped as fast as the flamingo. In the air the flamingo went like an arrow, resting not, although the blazing fire burned her neck and breast until it became pink and red. But that she heeded not.

Straight up the valley and to the rock where Natalia was bound went she, and into a heap of dried moss on the south side of the rock she dropped the blazing stick. Up leaped the dancing flames, and with a tremendous noise the rock flew into a thousand pieces and the power of the witch was gone for ever. As for Natalia, she was at once freed, and with her gentle, cool hand stroked the breast of the flamingo so that the burns were healed, but as a sign of its bravery the bird has carried a crimson breast from that day to this.

As for Natalia and Luis, they lived for many, many years in the valley, and about them birds of many kinds played and lived and reared their young, and the magic ball of the witch lived only in the memory of men.

Christmas Cherries

❧ *Elizabeth Janet Gray* ❧

Long ago in the days of our hardy and nimble ancestors, in the time of the great King Arthur's father, King Uther Pendragon, lived a knight called Sir Cleges. He was a tall man, fair and strong, and there wasn't a more courteous knight in all the world, or a more generous one. When squires came home poor from the wars, he gave them money and land; he was kind and comforting to his tenants; his house was open to all who came. His wife, whose name was Dame Clarice, was good and beautiful and blithe.

Every year at Christmas, Sir Cleges gave a feast, as royal a feast as if he had been king instead of a knight. Everybody in the countryside came to it, rich and poor, and minstrels were there to entertain them, trumpeters and pipers and drummers, harpers and lute-

73

players and fiddlers. The hall was full of carols and dancing, and there were rich meats and good drinks for all. When it was over Sir Cleges gave presents to the minstrels, gold and silver and rich robes, horses to ride.

Ten years or more he held such feasts, giving away his goods with both hands until his fortune began to slip away. He sold his rich manors, one after another, and his tenancies and wide lands. His friends and followers slipped away, too, and at last he and his wife and two children were left alone in a small manor near Cardiffside.

Christmas Eve came, and then was Sir Cleges sorrowful, indeed. He walked up and down and wrung his hands and groaned to think of the mirth he used to make at this time in honor of the King of Heaven. His wife came to him and put her arm through his and kissed him and tried to comfort him.

"My true love," she said softly, "it helps not a bit to go on lamenting. Let your sorrow go away. In this holy time every man should be merry and glad with what he has and thank God for it. Let us go in and have our dinner and be blithe as we can. I have cooked our meat carefully and I hope to your pleasure."

"Now I assent to that," Sir Cleges said, somewhat comforted. He put on an air of cheerfulness and quickly wiped away the tears that hung on his cheeks. They washed and went to eat, and when they had eaten, they played with their children till the bells rang for evensong.

After they came home from church, Sir Cleges sent his wife and children into the house before him and he went into the garden. There, on the cold, frost-hard ground, he knelt down under a bare cherry tree to pray. He thanked God with all his heart for all the poor and sorrowful people who had ever come to him to be helped. Though he had nothing to give now, he was thankful that once he had been able to spread joy and comfort at Christmas time.

As he got up from his knees he reached out and took hold of a branch of the cherry tree to steady himself. Then a wonderful thing happened. The cold bare branch under his hand put forth green leaves and round red berries.

"Dear Lord of Christmas," said Sir Cleges, "what kind of berries may these be, at this time of the year?"

He put one in his mouth. It was a ripe cherry, the best he had ever tasted since he was a little boy. He cut off a branch with leaves and cherries on it and brought it in his hand to show Dame Clarice.

"Look, wife, here is a novelty! Cherries on a tree in our garden! I am afraid it is a token, because of our great complaint, that more trouble is on the way."

"Nonsense!" said Dame Clarice. "It is a token of good things on the way. Whether we have less or whether we have more, let us always thank God for it. That's the best way, truly. Now," she went on, full of brisk cheer, "let us fill a basket with the fruit God sent us, and tomorrow morning early you shall take it to Cardiff to the king."

The next morning before daylight the lady had the basket full. She called her elder son and said, "Take up this basket and carry it on your back for your father."

Sir Cleges took a staff. Having no horses to ride now, he walked with a staff as poor men do. At noon he and his son came to the gate of the king's castle at Cardiff. When the porter saw them and their staffs and shabby clothes, he shouted angrily, "Get out of here, you! Go stand in the beggar's row or I'll break your heads for you!"

"Good sir," said Sir Cleges politely, "I pray you let us go in. I have brought the king a present from Him who made all things out of nothing."

The porter went to the basket and lifted up the lid. He saw the cherries. Cherries at Christmas time and the ground frozen hard! Well he knew the king would like such a present and would reward the giver.

"Through this gate you shall not go," he said, "unless you promise me a third of what the king gives you, silver, or gold, or whatever it is."

Sir Cleges agreed to that. What else could he do?

The porter opened the outer gate and into the courtyard went Sir Cleges and his boy. Before they could go into the great hall another officer met them, the usher who seats the guests at the king's table.

"Out of my sight, churl," cried the usher, "or I'll beat you, limb, head and body, without mercy."

"Good sir," said Sir Cleges, "don't be so angry. I have brought the king a present from Him who made everything out of nothing and died upon the Cross. Last night this fruit grew. Look at it and see if I speak the truth. It is fresh and sweet."

The usher lifted up the lid smartly and marveled at what he saw. "That may be," he said, "but I tell you truly, you don't come into this hall on your two feet unless you promise me a third part of whatever you get from the king."

Sir Cleges saw no other hope. He gave the second promise, and feeling a bit depressed he took his son and his basket and went on into the hall.

At once the steward came striding toward him, through the crowd of richly dressed lords and ladies, and stopped him. "Who made you so bold," he demanded "as to come here uninvited? This is no place for a churl in old clothes. I advise you to leave, and that quickly."

"Sir," said Sir Cleges patiently, "I have brought the king a present from that Lord that bought us dearly and died for us."

The steward pounced on the basket and plucked up the lid. "On my word," he said amazed. "Never in all my life have I seen cherries at this time of the year. You can't come near the king unless you promise to give me a third of whatever the king gives you. One third for me—or out you go, packing."

Sir Cleges stood and thought. "If I divide the king's gift among three men, there will be nothing left for me." He sighed.

"Come on," the steward prodded him. "Where's your tongue? Promise what I ask, or I'll take your stick and beat your rags into your back and shove you out of here headfirst!"

Sir Cleges saw no help for it. "Whatever the king rewards me with," he sighed, "you shall have a third of it, whether it be much or little."

As soon as he said that, the steward let him pass. He went up to the dais where the high table was, and kneeling before the king, uncovered the basket. Still kneeling, he said, "Our Saviour sent you this fruit which grew last night in my garden."

The king saw the fresh, ripe cherries, and he gave thanks reverently for them. Then he told Sir Cleges to go and get something to eat and to return afterward, without fail.

The king took some of the cherries himself, and sent some as a present to a gentle and lovely lady of Cornwall. (She later married him.) And the rest he served throughout the hall for all to taste.

When all the company was merry, the king bade a squire find the poor man who had brought the cherries. The squire went quickly, without any scorn for the staff and rags, and brought Sir Cleges to the high table.

"I thank you heartily," said the king, "for your rare present. You have honored all my guests with your dainties, and given me pleasure also. Whatever you would like to have, I'll grant you. Land, or servants, or other goods, whatever your heart yearns for, that you may have."

Sir Cleges had made three promises. Remembering them, he said: "Gramercy, my king! That is too great a gift for such a man as I. Land or servants or other goods—that is too much for me. But since I may choose for myself, I ask nothing but twelve blows with a staff."

Then answered King Uther, "Twelve blows, indeed! I repent of my promise. By Saint Charity, you had better take gold or land— you have more need of them."

Sir Cleges couldn't deny that, but still he said, "My lord, it is your own promise."

The king was angry and sorry, too, but he had to keep his word. The poor man who brought the cherries should have his twelve blows.

Then Sir Cleges straightened up, and he took his staff, and he strode down the hall among all the great lords. He sought out the steward first, to pay him his reward. He gave the steward four good thwacks, till that one begged, "Sir, for your courtesy, strike me no more."

Then out of the hall Sir Cleges went and found the usher. He gave him four such dunts that for many a day after that the usher denied no man entrance.

"By my thrift," said Sir Cleges, "now you've got the third part of my gift, just as you made me promise you."

Then he hurried to the porter and paid him his share. For many a day afterward that porter was courteous to all who came to the gate, whether on horseback or on foot.

When he had fulfilled his promises, Sir Cleges went back to the hall. He found the king and his lords and ladies listening to a harper telling a tale.

When it was finished, Sir Cleges heard the king say, "Minstrel, you have traveled far, and doubtless you have heard many things. Tell me if you know anything of that poor man who brought me cherries today."

The harper said, "My lord, he was a knight of yours once. Men called him Cleges."

"This is not he," said the king. "Sir Cleges died long ago. I loved him dearly. Would that he were here now! I would rather have him than three other knights."

Then Sir Cleges made his way among the knights and ladies and knelt before the king and thanked him politely for granting his wish. When the king asked him why he wanted what he did, and why he gave it away, he answered, "I could not come in till I promised each of those three a third of what you would give me. If I did that, I should have nothing myself. To divide twelve blows among them seemed best, truly."

The lords laughed, old and young; everybody around the king laughed; they laughed so hard they almost fell off their chairs.

The king said to Sir Cleges, "Tell me, good man, what is your name?"

And Sir Cleges told him.

"Are you my own knight, who was so gentle and generous, so strong, hardy and nimble?"

Then and there, the king gave Sir Cleges all that belongs to a knight. He made him steward of all his lands, besides. He gave him a golden cup to take to Dame Clarice. He made his son a squire. Then he let him go home to tell the good news.

Sir Cleges was a gentle steward; young and old loved him for his courtesy and kindness. His children grew up and prospered. He and his lady lived many a merry year after that, till God sent for them.

The General Did Wrong

≈[Jeanette Eaton]≈

At the crest of a steep hill three horses were pulled to a stop. Three riders, wearing blue coats, buff trousers, high boots and three-cornered hats, looked eagerly around. The tallest of them, twisting the reins about his wrist, lifted a pair of field glasses to his eyes and scanned woods and fields in every direction.

The youngest of the other two riders leaned toward him and burst out, "Tell us, General Washington, what you see! British scouts? Smoke of camp fires?"

Washington put down his glasses, shook his head and smiled. "Remember, Marquis, it will take enemy troops many days to march up the Delaware from their landing place." Then turning

80

to the man on his right, he said teasingly, "Nathaniel, the Marquis de Lafayette is more eager than we for battle."

General Nathaniel Greene, who had been in the army even longer than the Commander himself, smiled grimly. He said, "Sir, we've ridden over this region all day and haven't seen a single place where we could make a stand against the enemy."

"True enough, Nathaniel." Washington sighed.

"This beautiful land," Lafayette was saying, "is like my own France."

"True enough, Nathaniel," Washington sighed.

"But not good fighting country," said Washington briskly and gathered up the reins. "We'll take a look down by Brandywine Creek."

As they rode along a wooded path the Commander reviewed his problems. It was now late August 1777. In two years of leading the American Revolutionary Army he had had only one real victory. All the rest had been a horror of bloody defeats and shameful retreat. His army was always too small for attack.

Greene's voice cut across Washington's thoughts. "Look, General, we're in for a storm!"

The horsemen had come out of the woods upon a meadow. From the right a mountainous black cloud was sweeping toward them. Jagged lightning flashed from it and thunder shook the ground.

"Behold a house across the field!" shouted Lafayette. "Let us take shelter there, yes?"

"Yes. Forward!" Washington touched his horse's flank with spurs and led the dash to the farm house.

Another flash of lightning and roar of thunder! Just as the three reached the big stone barn, the rain came pouring down. They rode under a projecting roof and dismounted.

Lafayette laughed gaily. "Just in time, my General, to save your fine uniform!"

"And your brand new one, Marquis!" grinned Greene. But the smile left his face as a tall figure in homespun suddenly appeared in the barn.

The farmer was staring first at one and then the other of his visitors. "Officers of the Continental Army, eh?" he asked slowly.

Nathaniel searched the man's face. In this part of Pennsylvania lived many Tories. Here was Washington and two officers miles and miles from camp! Suppose this farmer were to sound an alarm to other Tories! What could prevent the capture of America's General-in-Chief?

In the farmer's eyes a vast amazement blazed up. "Why, it's General George Washington himself! Here on my farm! Sir, I saw you march your troops through Philadelphia a week ago. General, sir, you must come at once into the house. My wife will give you some refreshment. Our name is Small, sir!" He turned and shouted into the barn, "Tom, come take the gentlemen's horses. Rub them down, son, and water them!"

Washington, nodding in a friendly way, followed the farmer to the house. Lafayette followed the General. But Greene lingered. He wanted to be sure of things. What if the boy hid the horses? Then capture would be certain.

Tom, the farmer's son, was staring after the others. "Honest, is that the General?" he asked in an awed voice. "I never thought to see him. I wanted to enlist, but father said no, he needed me. Oh, if I could only join up!"

Greene listened carefully. Surely the boy wasn't pretending! But think of the reward offered for the General's capture! If only camp were not so far away! If only it weren't so late—almost six o'clock.

Aloud he said, "Well, boy, at least you groom the General's horse. Let me see where the stalls are!" He strode into the barn for a look. "All right, Tom, I'll be back later."

Through pelting rain Nathaniel ran to the house. In the big, clean kitchen the farmer's wife bustled about with pots and pans

and her husband was opening a jug of cider. Lafayette paced rest-
lessly from one window to the other. But Washington sat at the
table with long legs stretched out looking very much at ease.

Then with a glance out of the window the commander remarked,
"The rain will last for hours, I think. Could you good people let
us remain here for the night?"

Greene saw by Lafayette's start that he also was worried. Both
the Smalls, declaring they would be happy to serve, hurried upstairs to see about the beds.

Instantly Lafayette and Greene were beside Washington. "General," cried Nathaniel, "you can't stay here! What do you know of
these people? If they are Tories, sir, you'll be in British hands at
dawn!"

"Indeed, Your Excellency," chimed in the Frenchman, "this is
truth. Let us go back to camp, rain or no rain. To stay is risk!"

Washington said coldly, "We will stay."

For a time over the pleasant supper Nathaniel dropped his anxiety. Lafayette, talking a mile a minute, had evidently forgotten
his. Once they had all gone upstairs to bed, however, Greene's
fears came back. Without undressing, he lay on the blanket, kept
his pistol cocked and every few minutes went to the half-open
door to listen.

Just before dawn he heard a horse whinny. Then a dog barked.
Springing up, Nathaniel crept downstairs and out to the barn.
In the stalls, he found the horses safe and sound. He stepped to his
gray mare and laid his hand on her neck.

"Don't do it, sir!" A low, tense voice cut the darkness.

"Who's there?" Hand on pistol, Greene whirled around.

"Me! Tom Small! And I say don't run away, sir! Don't leave the
General!"

"Run away? What do you mean?"

The boy's feet shuffled in the straw. "Weren't you going to take
your horse and slip off? I've been here keeping watch."

"You fool!" shouted Greene. "You think me a traitor?"

"I feared it, sir. You seemed uneasy and—strange. I thought . . . there have been deserters a-plenty. Traitors, too."

Suddenly Greene burst into a roar of laughter. "Tom, you and I were uneasy for the same reason. When I heard a horse whinny, I came to see that nothing was wrong!"

"Is that so, sir?"

"You don't believe me? Well, boy, I'll stretch out in the hay beside you till sun-up and we'll both keep watch."

At breakfast two hours later, Washington looked up from his plateful of flannel cakes to say, "Nathaniel, you look as if you hadn't slept all night. What ails you, sir?"

Greene turned to wink at the boy standing by the stove and answered, "General, Tom Small and I were on sentry duty."

There was a flash in Washington's grey-blue eyes, but he said nothing.

After warm farewells to the Small family, the horsemen set off at a gallop. When they paused for rest, three abreast, Washington said, "Gentlemen you were right. I did take a risk to stay so far from camp. I was quite wrong."

Touched to the quick, Greene could only nod. But Lafayette flung out his hand in a gesture of homage. "Ah, my General, it is only a great man who will say, 'I was wrong.'"

The Elegant Snoop
(*Die Stultorum*)

°⟦ *William Hall* ⟧°

Upon a time once there was a man very neatly dressed in a blue suit, brown shoes and a brown necktie, not to mention his brown hat and his brown socks.

The man, so dressed, opened the front door of his house, looked under the doormat, in the mailbox and under the front porch. Then he pulled his hat further down on his head, retied his shoelaces to make them tighter and looked into the mouth of his dog who was sitting on the curb.

Just then the man's new limousine pulled up before him with his chauffer at the wheel, and the man and the dog jumped into the back seat. The man reached over and lifted up the chauffeur's cap, looked into it and replaced it on the chauffeur's head, pulling it well down over the driver's ears. Then the man and the dog jumped out of the car and it drove off.

You may think that such a well-dressed man would not be seen sitting on the curb with his shoes off, but he was. And he was looking way inside of them with the help of a little flashlight. Soon he put them back on, tying and retying them twice. He could never get them tied TIGHT enough.

After his shoes were nicely tied, he and the dog just sat there until a big truck drove up and out jumped three men with crowbars who commenced to pry up the flagstones of the sidewalk, one by one. As they raised one, the man and his dog peered under it and then the men replaced it. They raised twenty flagstones for the man and his dog to look beneath and then they lined up side by side. One by one, their hats were removed by the man and he looked into each, and replaced it carefully, pulling it well down over the workman's head. He hated to see hats not really ON.

The men climbed into the truck and away they went. The man opened the dog's mouth and looked into it, then the two of them walked off down the street.

Not long afterward the man and his dog were seen entering a furniture store. They went directly to the bedroom furniture department where the man proceeded to open the bureau drawers. He'd open one, look in, and shut it, beginning always with the bottom drawer of each bureau.

The dog found a soft bed, climbed up on it and went to sleep while the man spent the rest of the day looking into eight hundred and ninety bureau drawers.

Soon it was time for the furniture store to close and the manager came over to the man and asked him if he could help him find something.

The man replied that he had read this story that you're reading about him before and was looking for the ending, which was a fine answer considering that the date was April First.

Christmas in Summer

Charlotte Lohse

It was Sale Day in the first week of December when I heard about the Christmas party. That was the day Dad sold Betsy, the roan mare. I'll always remember it because I loved Betsy and I was feeling pretty low. I was eleven and a half, and the last two years I had been helping Dad drive the stock into Mooltana, a handful of a place in the far northern end of South Australia. It had been fun that morning, riding the mare through our township. It was a clear hot day. The sun glittered on the glossy young steers as they jostled each other along the narrow street, kicking up great clouds of dust and filling the quiet little town with noisy bawling.

The townspeople kept their children off the streets on Sale Day.

They were afraid of the long-horned flighty steers. But I rode right behind them, cracking my long whip and keeping them in order. Now and then Betsy reared up on her hind legs, and it was all exciting and sort of glorious.

But when I got in the hooded buggy to drive home with Mum, who had come in to do some shopping, it seemed all the good had gone out of the day. It was going to be awfully lonely without the roan mare. Mum gave me her special slow smile, but I knew she wasn't feeling happy either. You see I just rode Betsy to keep her in shape for Mum, because the roan really belonged to her. Sometimes I thought Mum cared more for Betsy than she did for Dad and me together.

Times were skimpy, and there'd been talk of selling Betsy for quite a while. The night before I'd heard Dad talking to Mum.

"If Old Man Riley offers a topnotch price perhaps we should sell."

Mum's voice was quiet. "Of course, Tim," she said to Dad, "I know Betsy is a luxury we can't afford these days. There are so many other things we need."

I fell asleep in my little room next to the kitchen thinking hopefully that Mr. Riley was a hard bargain-maker and that perhaps he wouldn't even be at the sale. He was, though, and he must have really wanted the mare because he paid a whopping good price for her. In spite of the money, I saw Dad's face when it happened, and it was as long as mine. I knew Dad would never have sold Betsy if there had been any other way.

Now I glanced up at Mum as she drove the gray ponies through the town. She was looking straight ahead, and I had the odd feeling that she was far away even though she was sitting right next to me.

When we came to the big brown house at the end of the street, Mum pulled up the grays. Doctor Brenner's house that was. "Little Doctor" we called him, and we loved him and brought him things from the farm whenever we came into town.

"Hop into the house," Mum said. "It's too late to visit. Give the doctor our regards and tell him we'll see him next Sale Day."

From under the buggy seat she got out a basket carefully covered with a big white tea towel and handed it to me. Eggs, clotted cream, cake and homemade sausages were inside. I'd helped Mum pack them early that morning.

I pulled out the shiny brass knob on the front door and let it spring back, listening to the harsh clangy sound it made echoing down the long passage. Little Doctor himself opened the door.

"Why, Timmie Holden," he said, "I haven't seen you for months. Where's the rest of your family? Aren't they coming in?"

I explained that we couldn't visit because Mum had a sick calf at home and we'd stayed too long at the sale already. And that Dad had had to stay in town.

"Well, anyway," he said, "I want to talk to your mother."

We went through the big front garden, out to the buggy. Little Doctor shook hands with Mum and asked about everyone in the family.

Then he said, "Look here, Mrs. Holden, we've made plans for a Christmas party for the children. I've asked everyone in the town, but I'd like the farm people to come in, too."

Mum said, "A Christmas party! Why, Doctor, I haven't thought about celebrating Christmas for years. Not since I left England."

Little Doctor's blue eyes twinkled. "That's what I thought," he said. "It's high time the children around here saw a Christmas tree. And that's another thing, Mrs. Holden; the best pine trees grow on that hill back of your place. Do you suppose big Tim and young Timmie here could bring in a tree a few days before Christmas?"

Mum's cheeks got pink the way they do when she's all stirred up. "Oh, I'm sure they could. A tall tree with thick wide branches. How high . . . how high could it be?"

Little Doctor laughed. You could see that he was pleased that Mum was so excited.

"Well," he said, "we're having the party in the Town Hall, so I think the tallest tree to be found would be all right." He mopped his face with a big handkerchief. "I hope the good Lord will send us a cool day for it," he said.

The grays were kicking up a fuss, anxious to be off.

"I say," Little Doctor called after us as we started off, "don't forget to get the news around. I want everyone to come."

Mum had often told me about Christmas in England, but I wanted to get everything fresh in my mind, so I had a million questions.

Our farm is fifteen miles north of Mooltana, so we had a long drive ahead of us. It was near sundown, but even when the sun was gone it would still be hot. The thermometer hadn't been below 102 degrees for weeks.

"This time of the year in England," Mum said softly, "it's cold, biting clear cold. When we children came in from school our cheeks and ears were stinging with the lovely icy cold." She sighed. "I'd love to feel that way just once again."

"Funny," I said, "freezing cold there and boiling hot here."

I thought how nice it would be to see the other side of the world where everything was different.

"Let me drive, Mum," I said, "you just talk."

The last bit of sun had slipped behind the faraway Flinders Range. It would be dark soon, but I knew I didn't have to worry about the grays. They knew the way and when they're heading for home they trot along at a good spanking pace.

"Snow falling," Mum said. "Oh, Timmie, some day you must see the snow fall, you must feel the thick soft soundless flakes against your face and watch them turn the world into a fairy tale."

It was black dark now, but soon the sky would be lit with stars. I like driving at night. The buggy wheels rolling and the clop-clop of the grays are part of the big quiet feeling that comes over me.

"A few days before Christmas," Mum went on, "a tall pine tree is set up inside the house, and all sorts of glittery pretty things hung on it with a golden angel on the topmost branch. All around the bottom of the tree presents are heaped, secret presents for everyone from everyone else."

For a while we stayed quiet. I thought about snow and Christmas trees and tidy small villages where people lived close to each other. Mum, I suppose, was thinking about when she was a little girl. Suddenly I wondered if she wished she were back in England, and I didn't like that thought at all. Then I started thinking about secret presents. I tasted the words in my mouth. Maybe . . . maybe there was some way I could give Mum a secret present for Christmas. Perhaps I could get Betsy back!

At the gate of the home paddock I gave Mum the reins and jumped down to open the gate. She sighed when I got back in the buggy.

"We should have kept up Christmas here," she said, "but it's always so hot, it just doesn't seem to belong."

That was Saturday, the third of December. Next day I had to ride over to the Rileys' for a special setting of eggs that Mrs. Riley had promised Mum. First off, of course, I told them about the party. Dora Riley, who is only seven, said "What's a Christmas tree?" I started to tell her, then suddenly I remembered that I didn't really know. She hung around, her black curls bobbing, her blue eyes wide, while I packed the eggs into my saddle bag.

"Ask your Granny about Christmas," I said. "She ought to know."

I suppose it seems queer that none of us knew about Christmas trees, but in the far north of South Australia it's hot most of the year. December is summertime, and the twenty-fifth often enough is a fair scorcher. So our families, who are all hard-working farmers, never bothered to celebrate.

As I got ready to swing into the saddle and get started home, Mr. Riley came out of the harness room with a bridle through his arm.

"Thought I'd try out the mare," he said. So I walked over to the stable paddock with him.

Sometimes Betsy made a fuss about being caught. I never had much trouble because I could sort of catch up with her, but Mr. Riley was heavy on his feet. Every time he got near the mare she frisked on her heels and got away. By the time he finally got the bridle on her, Mr. Riley was red and sweaty and his temper was short.

"Does she always act up that way?" he asked.

"Not always, Mr. Riley," I said.

Suddenly I felt a warm growing hope inside me. Mr. Riley was an all-right sort of person, and if I explained about a Christmas present for Mum, and if the mare kept on being troublesome . . . maybe Mr. Riley would sell her back to me.

You see, I had quite a bit of money of my own at home. My gran in England sent me a gold sovereign every birthday. Mum kept them in a little black tin box with a lock on it. When I was eight she gave me the key and told me the money was my responsibility. The shiny japanned box with gold lines painted round it was on my mind a lot, lying solidly underneath all the other things I thought about. I did whatever odd jobs I could to make more, and in the September Michaelmas Holidays I'd added quite a little to Gran's money by helping Mr. Riley fix his boundary fences.

Ever since I can remember I'd decided what I would do with the money when I had saved enough. I wanted a black mare that was really my own. I wanted to ride through the hills when the golden wattle was in flower. I wanted to take the high jumps in the stable paddock the way Mum did. I dreamed of the day I would enter my own horse in the Mooltana Show and take a couple of prizes. There was about enough money now in the tin box to buy a good horse, but this new idea of a surprise present for Mum sort of shunted the little black horse out of my mind.

School is only six miles from our place, so on Monday I managed to get there before the Rileys and tell the news first about the Christmas party. At playtime they all crowded around me.

"Yes," I said for the hundredth time, "everyone is invited. Little Doctor wants everyone to come."

Before Doctor Brenner settled in Mooltana, and that was only a few years ago, there wasn't a doctor within hundreds of miles. Most of the boys and girls had occasion to know him. He was what we called "square dinkum"—gentle and full of fun. You forgot to be scared even if a tooth had to be yanked out. So if Little Doctor was giving a party we all knew it would be something special.

Every playtime from that day was full of talk about it. The girls stood around under the big gum tree, whispering and giggling about what they were going to wear. We boys pitched horseshoes and took it in our stride.

Billie Riley said carelessly, "Be glad to help you chop down that pine for the Christmas tree. Pa said we could have the dray to take it in to Mooltana. Says he's got to see the Little Doctor anyhow."

Dad was extra busy. So Billie, Mr. Riley and I walked over every bit of the pine hill looking for the best tree. We found a beauty. It had thick outspread branches with fat brown cones on them and it was tall and strong. We sat down on some stumps and rested a while after we got it cut down. Now was my chance I thought. I watched Mr. Riley tamp down the tobacco in his pipe. After he got his smoke going I started to explain.

He listened quietly while I told him how badly Mum missed the roan mare, how she loved to ride.

"I know," he said. "Life here is kind of hard on your ma. Still and all, Timmie, I paid good money for the mare."

"I can give you a pound more than you paid for her," I said, trying to keep my voice steady, "and . . . I want very much to give Betsy to Mum for a Christmas present."

He looked at me for a moment and my heart sank to my boots.

"My gran in England sends me money every birthday you know, and. . . ."

"Yes, I know," he said. "Want to spend it on your ma, eh, Tim? Well," he grinned, "I've been losing my temper regular with that mare. It's a bargain, Timmie."

We shook hands on it. "If we could get Betsy into Mooltana today," I said, "Little Doctor would keep her in his stables till the party."

Back at the farm while Mr. Riley was talking to Dad, I dashed up to my room and emptied the sovereigns into a little canvas bag that usually carried my marbles, tying the open end with a piece of string. For a minute I felt a little sick inside. It would be a long time before I could think of owning a beautiful black horse and taking a prize at the show.

I rode Betsy into Mooltana from the Riley place, with Mr. Riley and Billie and the tree in the dray beside me. We stopped at the Little Doctor's house, and it was all right with him so I left Betsy in his stable the few days till Christmas. He got in the dray with us and helped get the tree into the Town Hall.

Billie's eyes popped at the piles of huge cardboard boxes stacked up at one end of the Hall.

"What d'you suppose?" he said in a loud whisper. But Little Doctor hurried us outside. "That's a fine tree you brought," he said. "I'm much obliged to you."

When I got home Mum had the bedroom all spread out with things from the old tin trunk, a small worried frown between her eyes. She was looking at some thin white stuff with pink rosebuds sprigged on it.

"This will make a lovely dress for little Dora Riley," she said, half to herself. That stuff had been a dress Mum had worn to the church social. I remember how pretty she'd looked. She was small as a minute and slim, and her eyes were deep, deep brown.

We were up before sunrise on the morning of the twenty-fourth.

Like a miracle it rained during the night. It was fine helping Mum with the farm chores. The earth looked as though it had just been scrubbed, and the scent steaming up from it was a strange lovely mixture of all growing things. The woodbine creeper was still trembly with raindrops and sweeter than honey. I stuck my nose into the cabbage rose by the back gate, and the pink squashy petals were wet and spicy.

I was helping Mum with the milking when the sun came up. The old gray kookaburra in the gum tree began to chuckle, then worked himself up to rowdy laughter, the way he always does at sunrise. "It won't be dusty driving in, and it will be cool all day," said Dad, who, tired as he was, had started to get interested in the party along with Mum and me.

We climbed into the double seater buggy a bit before one. We had to pick up some of the Rileys because they don't own a buggy big enough for all of them.

It was half-past five before we got to Mooltana and six before we had the horses unharnessed, and ourselves tidied up. Mum had made over one of Dad's old suits for me, and pressed one of Dad's old ties for him so it looked like new. Her green dress looked pretty with a new frill. We all felt quite handsome.

The Town Hall is just a plain wooden building. It's like a barn inside with wooden rafters, kerosene lamps swinging from the ceiling on long chains, and a raised wooden stage at one end. But it didn't look like itself when we got there that evening. All the bare windows were garlanded with gumtree branches. Chinese lanterns, dozens of them, were strung across the room. There was an all-over sound of voices and laughter, not loud but excited and happy. Little Doctor and Mrs. Brenner were being everywhere at once. And in the center of the room was the tree!

So that was a Christmas tree! I wanted to sit by myself and really look at it. It reached almost to the ceiling, and hundreds of little white wax candles were perched on the branches. Packages in bright colored paper dangled, and heaps of them were piled around the bottom. The golden angel was there too, just as Mum had told me, floating on the top branch as though she watched over the whole thing.

After Little Doctor was sure we were all there he got up on the stage and told us how he'd tried to make the tree like the one he'd had as a boy. "Only thing," he said, "I couldn't manage the snow for outdoors."

Well, then the presents were given out. They'd been ordered weeks before from Adelaide over three hundred miles away. There were presents for everyone and some left over. Tops, paint boxes, balls, books, cricket bats, pocket knives, dolls, sewing sets, doll furniture. . . . The sighs and the o-ohs and the a-ahs went around the room in waves.

Dora Riley came running over to me with a china doll. "Look, Timmie, she's got a petticoat, shoes and a hat and drawers . . . and they all come off."

I got Kipling's *Jungle Book* (Little Doctor knew I was keen about Kipling) and a big bag of marbles.

After the presents were given out, Tim Mahoney, the constable, and Dad climbed on ladders and lit the little candles on the tree.

"Looks as though the stars came down to roost, Timmie," Mum said. But I didn't want to talk.

Later Dad came over and sat beside us. "I've something special for you, Timmie," he said, sort of awkwardly. I unwrapped the box he handed me, and inside was a heavy round glass ball with a green Christmas tree painted inside. When I turned it upside down the inside was filled with whirling tiny white blobs. "So you'll know about snow falling," Dad said.

It was beautiful. And to know Dad had had Dr. Brenner get it for him when he sent for the other presents! I turned it and turned it and thought I would never get tired of looking at it.

"Mum," I said looking up. But Mum's eyes were filled with tears.

Suddenly I felt heavy inside me and I thought again, "Mum wants to live in England; she doesn't really like it here."

We had supper—sandwiches, milk, cocoa, cake, and little biscuits with "hundreds and thousands" sprinkled on top of them. We were the last to leave and Doctor Brenner, who was at the door saying good night to everyone, walked with us to where Dad was harnessing the horses to the buggy in the Town Hall paddock. And there standing by the buggy was Betsy. Little Doctor put his arm round my shoulders. I was shaking with excitement. Then he shoved me forward gently. I went over to the mare and handed the reins to Mum.

"It's my Christmas present, Mum," I said. "I bought her back for you."

"Betsy," Mum said softly, "darling Betsy." Then she turned to me. "But I don't understand, Timmie . . . it's not possible, how could you?" Then after a minute she said, "Oh, Timmie, Gran's money . . . you spent Gran's money for me. The money that was to buy the little black horse. Timmie, Timmie."

"Gosh, Mum," I said, feeling awkward and funny about it. "I'd rather have Betsy round anyway."

Then Dad was there and the slow look he gave me told me he was pleased with what I'd done.

But Mum bent down and kissed me and her cheek was wet against mine.

Billie Riley rode the mare to our farm and planned to spend the night with us. I sat on the back seat of the buggy with Mum, as Mr. Riley was up front with Dad. She tucked her arm around me.

"Such a lovely, lovely evening, wasn't it, Timmie?" Mum said.

I leaned against her. "Mum," I said because I still wasn't sure, "if you could live anywhere you wanted, where would you choose?"

For a second there wasn't a sound. Then Mum started to laugh, a happy bubbling sound.

"What a foolish, foolish question, Timmie love," she said. "Only one place of course. I chose it long ago; right here on the farm with you and your father . . . and Betsy. You've been worrying about those tears back at the party. They were happy ones. But, oh, Timmie, I did miss Betsy. It was silly of me, but you've made everything perfect." I could feel her looking at me seriously. "I love Australia, too, Timmie, even though I wasn't born here."

I cupped the glass between my hands and wished that particular moment would last forever.

The Southern Cross sprawled big and brilliant against the sky. The buggy wheels, the trotting grays and Betsy's clip-clop behind us melted into nothingness.

Next thing I knew Mum was shaking me gently. "Wake up, Timmie dear," she said, "and help your father with the horses. We're home again, and it's Christmas Day."

Candles at Midnight

❀[*Alice Geer Kelsey*]❀

Now that he was ten, Costas Papadopoulos remembered very little about that long-ago time when he was only five. He had little in common with the small boy who thought he was hungry if dinner was ten minutes late and who thought that soldiers were only for parades. But in spite of all Costas had learned about hunger and enemy soldiers, during the last five years in Athens, there was one thing he did remember very clearly and very often. He could never forget the promises of the night before Easter, 1940.

"Next year you will be old enough to go," his father had promised him, speaking loudly because of the clanging of all the church

99

bells of Athens. "It is enough this year for you to come up here on our flat roof at midnight to watch."

"And shall I have fireworks to set off?" Costas had asked. His eyes had sparkled at the red, green, and gold of the Roman candles and rockets hissing and popping from Mt. Lycabettus and other hills about Athens.

"We shall stand together on the highest rock of Mt. Lycabettus to fire our rockets," Kyrios Papadopoulos had promised his son.

"And shall I have a candle to carry?" Costas had asked. His eyes danced from one place to another, as people at all churches in Athens were obeying the midnight bells and lighting their Easter candles. His eyes raised again to Mt. Lycabettus where the bell of St. George's chapel was ringing in triumph. The top of the mountain was blossoming in tiny golden flames as lights were passed from one candle to another. "Shall I have a long, white candle to carry from the top of Mt. Lycabettus?"

"Of course you will!" his mother had promised. "And you will shield it with your hand so carefully that it will stay lighted all the time that you walk the winding path down the mountain and through the streets home. That will bring you good luck all the year."

Four Easters had passed since then, but there had been no midnight fireworks nor long, white candles for Costas. The spring when Costas was six, his father had been in the Greek army fighting in the mountains. The Easters when he was seven and eight and nine, there had been conquering soldiers in Athens, insisting that each Greek be in his own house early every evening.

Now that Costas was ten, beautiful Athens was free again. Often during that sunny week before Easter, 1945, Costas had climbed the twisting stairway to his roof to get a better look at Mt. Lycabettus. At almost any time, he could see the tiny figures of people toiling up the hill to say their Holy Week prayers in the gleaming, white-washed chapel of St. George at the summit.

"You are old enough to go alone now, Costas," his father said to him on the day before Easter.

"Yes, Father!" The boy understood why his father could not go with him. It had been four years now that Kyrios Papadopoulos had been out of the army and walking painfully with a cane. The long climb up Mt. Lycabettus would be hard for him at any time —quite impossible as part of the gay Easter crowd.

"I will watch from the roof," smiled the father. "Point your rockets over this house. Then I will know which are yours."

"All right," grinned Costas, who could feel the fireworks in his fingers already. "And the long, white candle—I will carry it carefully all the way down the mountain and through the streets. I will climb up to our roof and give it to you still burning."

"You can try," smiled his mother.

"I *will* do it!" said Costas. "And bring you good luck for a whole long year."

"I am sorry not to have more money for fireworks and candles for you." Kyrios Papadopoulos opened his thin pocketbook and slowly counted out some worn paper money. "Two hundred drachmas is all we can possibly spare. That would have been plenty before the war. Prices are higher now. I hope it will be enough."

"You need spend nothing for Easter eggs." His mother pointed at the basket of blood-red eggs on the table. "You can carry two in your pocket. When the bells ring at midnight, you will want to crack eggs with the other boys."

"I will go to the market now to buy the candle and the fireworks." Costas was out the door and racing down the narrow street toward the wide streets, beyond which lay the market place. Not far from his own house, he saw a man with a push cart, selling candles.

"How much?" asked Costas.

"Fifty drachmas for the short brown ones. Two hundred drachmas for the long white ones," droned the candle-seller.

"But the short ones would not burn all the way down Mt. Lyca-bettus!" wailed Costas.

"The long ones will—only two hundred drachmas," droned the candle-seller. His eyes were already on a woman who looked as though she had more money.

"But then there would not be anything left for buying fire-works!" groaned Costas.

The candle-seller shrugged his shoulders. He turned toward the young woman who held out money for three long white candles.

Costas went slowly on. Perhaps if he went on toward the market streets, candles would be cheaper. He passed a man standing on the sidewalk holding a tray of fireworks.

"How much?" asked Costas.

"Fifty drachmas." The man pointed at some puny little fire-crackers. "One hundred drachmas. One hundred and fifty. Two hundred." He pointed to fireworks that grew bigger with the bigger prices. The one for two hundred was a beauty.

Costas shuffled slowly on toward the market place near the foot of the ancient Acropolis. Some days he loved to gaze dreamily at the stately Parthenon and the dainty Temple of Victory outlined against the sky. But today he was wondering merely if, where there were many salesmen, prices would be lower.

"How much?" he asked of candle-salesmen with trays, with baskets, with pushcarts.

"Fifty for the short brown ones. Two hundred for the long white ones." The answer was always the same.

"How much?" he asked of men selling candles in the sidewalk kiosks or in the stores.

"Fifty for the short brown candles. Two hundred for the long white ones."

"How much?" Costas asked of the candle salesmen sitting at tables beside the doors of churches.

"Fifty for the short brown ones. Two hundred for the long white ones."

Costas soon found it did no good to explain to the candle-sellers that he had only two hundred drachmas with which he must buy at least one rocket and a long white candle that would burn all the time that it took him to climb down Mt. Lycabettus, walk to his own house, and mount the stairs to his father's roof. The candle-salesmen were always busy selling to someone whose drachmas did not have to spread so far. Costas looked enviously at grimy bootblacks and ragged water-boys who could earn money of their own to spend.

It was nearly dark when Costas carried a long, slim, newspaper-wrapped parcel into the one big room that was home for himself and his parents. Tired, he flung himself onto the bed, under the picture of his father in uniform, while his mother put the plain supper on the table. This was the last of the fast-day meals. At midnight, with the cracking of the blood-red Easter eggs, the feasting would begin. Tomorrow there would be roast lamb and Easter sweets.

"Did you find the candle and fireworks?" asked his mother.

"Yes." But Costas did not offer to unroll his long, slim parcel.

"I wish I could climb Mt. Lycabettus with you tonight," said his mother, laying crunchy chunks of dark brown bread at each place. "But you know how hard it is for your father to be lame. I will watch with him from the roof. I will wait with him for you to come up the stairs to us with the last flickers of your tall, white Easter candle."

"Yes, Mother." Costas fingered the parcel. He started to say something. Just then his mother whisked out into the courtyard to draw cool water for the table. Costas said nothing.

Supper over, he rested a while, his paper parcel clutched tightly.

"Ten o'clock," called his father. "It's time to get ready to start up Mt. Lycabettus. You will want plenty of time to go into the chapel before midnight."

Costas rubbed sleepy eyes. He staggered out into the courtyard where, with a gourd, he dipped water from a big barrel to pour over his head, his hands, his feet. It was already warm enough to begin saving wear on shoes.

Costas went back to the table in the one big room. He chose two large blood-red eggs to stuff in his trouser pockets. He lifted the long paper parcel carefully and started for the door.

"We will be up on the roof when the bells begin to ring at midnight," promised his mother. "We will be watching the fireworks and the candles till you come climbing up the stairs with your burning candle."

Costas stood in the doorway as though there was something he wanted to say. He turned his long parcel slowly in his hand. He cleared his throat—but all that came was, "Good-by, Father. Good-by, Mother." He turned and went out alone into the night.

Costas had climbed Mt. Lycabettus often in the daytime, but never before in the middle of the night. He dodged through one dark, narrow street after another until one street ended in a long flight of stone steps. Then a turn to the left and he was on the broad road which hairpinned through the pines for the lower stretches of the trail up the mountainside. Then he turned off onto the path that zigzagged back and forth between the giant cactus plants, ascending little by little the steep sides of Lycabettus.

He could not leap ahead at his own speed because the path was filled with people climbing slowly, up and up. This gave more time to look down at the twinkling lights of the sprawling city. Where the loop made broad spots in the trail, salesmen of candles and fireworks had set up their little tables. Costas stopped by one and watched a bent little woman buy a short brown candle. He stopped by the next one and saw a well-dressed man count out two hundred drachmas for a tall white candle. He noticed that the fireworks were practically all sold out. He shifted his paper parcel to his other hand and climbed on up the looping path.

At the top of the mountain, he wriggled through the crowd around the door of the chapel. Inside there were soft lights burning before sacred pictures. The long-haired priest in his black robes was chanting with the choir while people moved quietly in and out of the chapel. Everywhere was the thick fragrance of incense.

Costas did not linger long. He wanted to be on top of the highest point of Mt. Lycabettus when the midnight bells should announce that Easter had arrived. He went outside and climbed the high wall that edged the enclosure east of the chapel. He could look down at the lights of all Athens and Piraeus. He could see even the twinkle of the big lanterns on fishermen's boats out in the harbor.

Mt. Hymettus rose dark behind him. Gleaming golden over the city were the ancient temples of the Acropolis, now bathed in flood lights in honor of Holy Week. Above him, the stars seemed almost close enough to touch.

Far below, the deep bell of the great Metropolitan Church rang out clearly. It was midnight. All over the city, bells sprang to life. A joyous clanging rose from all the churches, celebrating at once the Resurrection of their Lord and the new freedom of their country. So thrilled was Costas with the triumphant chorus of bells that he quite forgot to break his blood-red eggs on those of the boys standing near him. It was only the snapping and hissing of fireworks and the lighting of candles that reminded him that he, too, had a part in the celebration.

He discarded the newspaper wrapping and stood looking at his treasures—a long and beautiful rocket and a short brown candle. He looked in shame at the little candle made of the cheap dark tallow which burned so quickly.

"If I do not light it until I am almost home, they will never know," he tried to comfort himself. But the plan that had seemed all right in the market place seemed all too shabby under the stars, with the bells ringing joyously all about him, and the people singing with the priest the praises of the Risen Lord.

Fireworks were going off on every side, with people dodging them and laughing excitedly. Children were cracking eggs together, each trying to prove his the stronger egg. In an attempt to forget the smallness of his brown candle, Costas raised his rocket high over his head. He lighted a match that sputtered and went out. He struck a second match. He almost touched it to the rocket—but paused.

All around the people were lighting their tall white candles for the march home. As long as the rocket was unspent, there was still a chance to change his mind. He listened to the bells of triumph. He heard the people chanting, "Christ is risen. He is risen indeed."

Costas held the rocket high over his head. In a small voice that could scarcely be heard for the shouting about him, he called, "Rocket for sale. Skyrocket for sale. Two hundred drachmas." He waited and listened.

"I'll take it," said a voice close by. "I tried to buy some for my little Yiannis on the way here, but they were all sold."

Costas clung to his beautiful rocket for a moment. Then he handed it over, lingeringly, to the tall man who counted out four fifty-drachma notes.

"Would you mind," asked Costas in a tight, thin voice, "letting me stand near by while Yiannis sets off the rocket?"

The rocket sputtered and sailed high over the heads of the crowd. As it flickered out, Costas' eyes were drawn by candle processions around other churches far below in the city. Then, grasping his two hundred drachmas in his hand, Costas wriggled his way through the crowd to the table by the chapel door where candles were sold.

"A long white candle," called Costas, laying down the four crumpled fifty-drachma notes with a glad flourish.

The candle-seller picked from the tray a candle that was truly beautiful in its tall, slim whiteness. The black-robed priest himself, smiling through his curly black beard, stooped to light Costas' candle. From the white candle, Costas lighted his short brown one. He pushed his way into the little chapel and placed a small candle before a picture of the Virgin Mary and the baby Jesus.

Then, proudly, Costas joined the happy throng that was chanting its way down the mountainside, each person carrying a lighted candle.

"Christ is risen!" they greeted each other.

"He is risen indeed!" was the answer.

Costas did not care if the procession was slow. Wasn't his the longest, whitest candle ever carried by a boy on an Easter midnight? It would surely burn for every stately step down the mountainside, and for the quick walk through the narrow dark streets to his own home.

Singing and carrying his candle high, Costas pushed open his courtyard gate. One inch of candle left! Singing louder, he climbed the winding iron stairs to the roof. Three-quarters of an inch of candle left! The flame breathed hotly on his fingers as he crossed the roof to where his father sat. Half an inch of burning candle he thrust into his father's waiting hands.

"Christ is risen!" greeted Costas.

"He is risen indeed!" answered his parents.

Gifts for the First Birthday

○〚 Ruth Sawyer 〛○

There is a people who are called wanderers; some say they have been wanderers for two thousand years. Now, they are vagabonds, for the most part, dirty thieving rascals, ready to tell a fortune or pick a pocket, as the fancy takes them; but—it was not always so. Some say that they have been cursed because they feared to give shelter to Mary and Joseph and the Child when the King of Judea forced them to flee into Egypt. But the gipsies themselves say that this is not true; and this is the story the gipsy mothers tell their children on the night of Christmas, as they sit around the fire that is always burning in the heart of a Romany camp.

It was winter—and twelve months since the gipsies had driven their flocks of mountain-sheep over the dark, gloomy Balkans, and had settled in the southlands near to the Ægean. It was twelve months since they had seen a wonderful star appear in the sky and heard the singing of angelic voices afar off.

They had marveled much concerning the star until a runner had passed them from the South bringing them news that the star had marked the birth of a Child whom the wise men had hailed as "King of Israel" and "Prince of Peace." This had made Herod of Judea both afraid and angry and he had sent soldiers secretly to kill the Child; but in the night they had miraculously disappeared —the Child with Mary and Joseph—and no one knew whither they had gone. Therefore Herod had sent runners all over the lands that bordered the Mediterranean with a message forbidding every one giving food or shelter or warmth to the Child, under penalty of death. For Herod's anger was far-reaching and where his anger fell there fell his sword likewise. Having given his warning, the runner passed on, leaving the gipsies to marvel much over the tale they had heard and the meaning of the star.

Now on that day that marked the end of the twelve months since the star had shone the gipsies said among themselves: "Dost thou think that the star will shine again tonight? If it were true, what the runner said, that when it shone twelve months ago it marked the place where the Child lay it may even mark His hiding-place this night. Then Herod would know where to find Him, and send his soldiers again to slay Him. That would be a cruel thing to happen!"

The air was chill with the winter frost, even there in the south-land, close to the Ægean; and the gipsies built high their fire and hung their kettle full of millet, fish, and bitter herbs for their supper. The king lay on his couch of tiger-skins and on his arms were amulets of heavy gold, while rings of gold were on his fingers and in his ears. His tunic was of heavy silk covered with a leopard cloak, and on his feet were shoes of goat-skin trimmed with fur. Now, as they feasted around the fire a voice came to them through the darkness, calling. It was a man's voice, climbing the mountains from the south.

"Ohe! Ohe!" he shouted. And then nearer, "O—he!"

The gipsies were still disputing among themselves whence the voice came when there walked into the circle about the fire a tall, shaggy man, grizzled with age, and a sweet-faced young mother carrying a child.

"We are outcasts," said the man, hoarsely. "Ye must know that whosoever succors us will bring Herod's vengeance like a sword about his head. For a year we have wandered homeless and cursed over the world. Only the wild creatures have not feared to share their food and give us shelter in their lairs. But tonight we can go no farther; and we beg the warmth of your fire and food enough to stay us until the morrow."

The king looked at them long before he made reply. He saw the weariness in their eyes and the famine in their cheeks; he saw, as well, the holy light that hung about the child, and he said at last to his men:

"It is the Child of Bethlehem, the one they call the 'Prince of Peace.' As yon man says, who shelters them shelters the wrath of Herod as well. Shall we let them tarry?"

One of their number sprang to his feet, crying: "It is a sin to turn strangers from the fire, a greater sin if they be poor and friendless. And what is a king's wrath to us? I say bid them welcome. What say the rest?"

And with one accord the gipsies shouted, "Yea, let them tarry!"

They brought fresh skins and threw them down beside the fire for the man and woman to rest on. They brought them food and wine, and goat's milk for the Child; and when they had seen that all was made comfortable for them they gathered round the Child —these black gipsy men—to touch His small white hands and feel His golden hair. They brought Him a chain of gold to play with and another for His neck and tiny arm.

"See, these shall be Thy gifts, little one," said they, "the gifts for Thy first birthday."

And long after all had fallen asleep the Child lay on His bed of skins beside the blazing fire and watched the light dance on the beads of gold. He laughed and clapped His hands together to see the pretty sight they made; and then a bird called out of the thicket close by.

"Little Child of Bethlehem," it called, "I, too, have a birth gift for Thee. I will sing Thy cradle song this night." And softly, like the tinkling of a silver bell and like clear water running over mossy places, the nightingale sang and sang, filling the air with melodies.

And then another voice called to him:

"Little Child of Bethlehem, I am only a tree with boughs all bare, for the winter has stolen my green cloak, but I also can give Thee a birth gift. I can give Thee shelter from the biting north wind that blows." And the tree bent low its branches and twined a rooftree and a wall about the Child.

Soon the Child was fast asleep, and while He slept a small brown bird hopped out of the thicket. Cocking his little head, he said:

"What can I be giving the Child of Bethlehem? I could fetch Him a fat worm to eat or catch Him the beetle that crawls on yonder bush, but He would not like that! And I could tell Him a story of the lands of the north, but He is asleep and would not hear." And the brown bird shook its head quite sorrowfully. Then it saw that the wind was bringing the sparks from the fire nearer and nearer to the sleeping Child.

"I know what I can do," said the bird, joyously. "I can catch the hot sparks on my breast, for if one should fall upon the Child it would burn Him grievously."

So the small brown bird spread wide his wings and caught the sparks on his own brown breast. So many fell that the feathers were burned; and burned was the flesh beneath until the breast was no longer brown, but red.

Next morning, when the gipsies awoke, they found Mary and Joseph and the Child gone. For Herod had died, and an angel had come in the night and carried them back to the land of Judea. But the good God blessed those who had cared that night for the Child.

To the nightingale He said: "Your song shall be the sweetest in all the world, for ever and ever; and only you shall sing the long night through."

To the tree He said: "Little fir-tree, never more shall your branches be bare. Winter and summer you and your seedlings shall stay green, ever green."

Last of all He blessed the brown bird: "Faithful little watcher, from this night forth you and your children shall have red breasts, that the world may never forget your gift to the Child of Bethlehem."

The Truce of the Wolf

Mary Gould Davis

In Gubbio, seven hundred years ago, the winter had been a hard one. Snow had fallen more than once, and in the deep ravine that separated the two mountains behind the town the bitter, merciless winds had howled and raged day after day. Never in the history of Gubbio had the wolves been so bold and so determined. The citizens, armed with rocks and heavy staves, had risen in the night to drive them away, again and again; but night after night they returned, stealing the sheep and the young kids, raiding the hen-houses, coming boldly inside the great walls that were built to keep them out. Matteo, the baker and the strongest and bravest

113

man in the town, said that their boldness was partly due to leadership.

"There is one great one who fears nothing," he told the anxious *padre*. "He catches the stones that we throw in his teeth and grinds them to powder. He comes so silently that you do not know he is there until you feel his breath on your shoulder. He is a devil, *Padre*. He is the Devil himself in a wolf's form."

The *padre* sighed. "Then we must pray to the saints to deliver us," he answered sadly.

One day, just after the New Year, the two little daughters of Gemma, the laundry woman who lived near the great gate that led out into the ravine, went outside the gate to cut some dried heather for the donkey's bed. As dusk began to fall Gemma watched anxiously for their return. Finally she sent word to Matteo, who gathered some men about him and, passing through the gate, climbed the hill toward the caves where the wolves dwelt. Just outside the cave they saw in the fading light a little red shawl and, father on, a piece of the blue woolen dress that the older girl had been wearing. The sound of their footsteps brought from the dim shadows of the cave a snarl that made even Matteo start back. He knew that it was hopeless to attack the wolves in their own stronghold. And he knew, too, that it was too late to save the little girls. A shuddering horror swept through the town when the news became known. Mothers forbade their children to go beyond the house door, and every glimpse of Gemma's worn face brought a stab of pain and fear to the hearts of the women of Gubbio.

Late in the winter, when the courage and patience of every citizen was at its breaking point, Gino, Matteo's eldest son, staggered into the town at dusk supported on either side by one of his companions and bleeding from a great gash in his neck and shoulder. Tired out with his long day in the fields, he had thrown himself down under an olive tree to sleep, and had waked to find the great beast at his throat. The three boys had had a terrible struggle to beat the wolf off. He had resisted them like a mad thing until a well-aimed blow from Alfredo's mattock had driven him limping away. Gino's wound festered, and when—weeks later—he came among them again his right arm hung withered and useless at his side. The evening of the attack, when the day's work was over, a meeting was held in the square of the city. Every one in Gubbio who could walk was there, men and women and children clinging fearfully to their mothers' skirts. Mounting the pedestal of the fountain where all could see him, Matteo made an impassioned speech, reciting again the long list of the crimes of the great wolf, waking in the mind and heart of every one anger and fear and grief.

"We must go to the *podestà* and ask for soldiers," he shouted. "Alone, we have failed to catch and punish this great one. We must forget our pride and ask for outside help. We *must* have peace!"

The crowd murmured in assent, the murmur rising to a sort of roar as Gemma came through the square and sat down on the pedestal at Matteo's feet. Then from the door of the church where he had been listening the *padre* came, and the people parted to let him through. He mounted the pedestal beside Matteo, who instantly stepped down, leaving the *padre's* head and shoulders outlined in the fading light and visible to them all. His slow, silvery voice, the voice that they had listened to and obeyed for so many years, seemed to clear the troubled air and to bring with it an accustomed authority and calm.

"My people," said the *padre*, "before we send word to the soldiers, before we ask help for Gubbio from the *podestà*, let us seek the advice of Brother Francis of Assisi. You have all heard of him. You know what he has done for the troubled ones of his own town and all through Umbria. You know of his power over the beasts. It is said that they understand and even talk to him, and that he is absolutely without fear of even the wildest of them. Let us ask Brother Francis to come here to Gubbio. Let us put our trouble in his hands and abide by his decision."

Matteo shook his head doubtfully, and the *padre* turned to him with a little pleading gesture.

"It will mean only a little delay, Matteo," he said. "We can send a message to Assisi today. If Brother Francis can do nothing— then we must, of course, send for the soldiers." The *padre's* words carried great weight with the people. Matteo could see by their faces that they wanted to try his plan. He nodded.

"*Si, si, Padre,*" he said almost cheerfully. "We will send for Brother Francis and see what he can do—but in my heart I fear that he can do nothing."

That very night a messenger started across the valley to Assisi, and one day a few weeks later, when spring had unfurled the gray leaves of the olive trees, when the early crocus had spread its mantle of pale lavender over the hills, a little band of brown-clad Brothers made its way up the steep hill that led to the square of Gubbio. The *padre* was waiting for them at the church door, and when he saw Brother Francis' face, hope leaped like a flame in his heart. Rapidly, omitting nothing, he told the story of the wolf and his sins, and Brother Francis listened, a little shadow stealing into his serene eyes.

"I understand," he said when the *padre* had finished. "But if this one wolf truly is the leader and controls the others, then *he* must be made to understand. You have met him with fear and with violence. You must meet him without fear, and you must reason with him. You must tell him, without anger, that he is a thief and a murderer."

"But no one of us, or even no group of us, dares to go near enough to this wolf to tell him anything!" the *padre* answered a little ruefully.

Brother Francis smiled. Then he rose and gathered his brown robe about him.

"Then I will tell him," he said quietly.

Matteo, who was standing near with a number of the men of Gubbio, protested.

"You cannot go outside the gate alone, Brother Francis," he said. "If you go, you must take us all with you. The wolf will certainly try to murder you, and only our staves and our stones can save you."

Brother Francis shook his head.

"Your staves and your stones have failed," he answered. "I will try another way now, and I go alone. My brothers may follow at a little distance—if they are not afraid. But no man of Gubbio must come outside the gate while I am on the hillside." And the men fell back before the quiet authority of his voice.

With the group of friars a little way behind him, Brother Francis went steadily through the gate and turned up the hill toward the caves. The sun was at its setting, and the near hill was in deep shadow while the one across the ravine was bathed in a light so concentrated, so golden, that in it the budding genestra was like points of living flame. Brother Francis stepped into the shadow and went straight up to the entrance of the first cave. There was a large stone near this entrance, and here Francis sat himself down, gathering his robe about him and turning his face toward the mouth of the cave.

"Brother Wolf," he said, "come out into the light. I would like to see and talk to you."

There was no answer from the cave. But in its shadow two eyes burned like two tiny green flames. . . . The sun sank lower. The swallows swooping overhead flew in ever narrowing circles and finally came to rest on Francis' arm and shoulder, whistling faintly.

"Be still, little brothers," said Francis softly. And the birds were still.

The friars, grown bolder in the silence, drew nearer, and Brother Leo started toward the mouth of the cave. Instantly there came a snarl, and out of the shadows sprang the great wolf. His eyes burned, his fangs showed white in his gaping red mouth, the short gray hairs stood out in a ruffle around his neck. Quickly Francis lifted his hand and made the sign of the Cross. The great beast seemed to pause almost in mid-air; then he sank down beside the cave and laid his head on his crossed paws like a dog, his teeth still bared.

"If you are afraid, Brother Leo," said Francis, "move off behind the trees. There is no place for fear here." Then he turned again to the wolf.

"Brother Wolf," he said, and now the gentleness was gone from his voice and it was clear and resonant, "Brother Wolf, you have done much harm in the city of Gubbio. You have destroyed God's creatures without His leave. And not only have you slain and devoured beasts, you have also dared to kill and to destroy children. who are made in the image of God. Therefore you are a murderer and worthy of the gallows, and the hand of every man in the city is against you."

He paused for a moment, and his eyes studied the huge, gaunt figure before him. He saw how every bone showed through the rough gray coat, how the short ears were scarred with many desperate battles. The green eyes were still blazing with hate and suspicion.

"But I, Brother Wolf," Francis went on more gently, "would fain make peace between you and the men of Gubbio. I would make a truce and a contract that you shall injure them no more and that they shall forgive you all your sins."

The wolf lifted his head. For a long time Francis gazed steadily at him. Slowly, slowly the fire died out of the green eyes, and there remained in them only a great hunger. Francis' face softened. Well he knew what hunger did to beasts—and to men.

"If, Brother Wolf," he went on steadily, "if it pleases you to make and to observe a peace between you and the people of Gubbio, I promise to obtain for you the cost of your maintenance from the men of the city, so that you shall never again go hungry.

For well do I know that it is hunger that has driven you to these evil courses. But I beg of you now this grace. I ask your promise, Brother Wolf, that you will never do hurt again either to man or to beast. Will you promise me this?"

The lids drooped over the hungry eyes; the wolf bowed his head and made with his whole body a movement of acquiescence.

"Then, Brother Wolf," said Francis, and now his smile was like light in a dark place, "pledge me this promise, so that I may have full trust in you."

Francis held out his hand, and the great beast, rising, lifted his paw and laid it in the hand stretched out to meet it.

Francis got to his feet. His voice was as clear as a bell.

"I command you, Brother Wolf," he said, "to come now with me, fearing nothing, and we will confirm this peace before the people of Gubbio and in the Name of God."

The sun had sunk below the horizon and the valley was filled with a soft blue dusk as Francis, with the wolf at his side, his narrow gray head pressed against the brown robe, entered the city gate, the little band of friars following them. In the square the people of Gubbio—men and women and children—waited in breathless suspense for the return of the man from Assisi. As he appeared in the great portal with the shadowy form that they dreaded pressing close at his heels, a low murmur of amazement ran through the crowd. Francis passed straight on to the pedestal of the fountain, one hand resting lightly on the wolf's head. His voice, when he spoke, had in it a curious quality—the clear, joyous tone that you hear sometimes in the voice of a happy child.

"Hear me, people of Gubbio," he said. "Brother Wolf, who is here before you, has promised and pledged me his faith to make peace with you, never to injure you or harm you again in any way whatsoever. For your part you must promise him his daily sustenance in winter and in summer throughout the year. And I am bondsman for him, that he will keep and preserve through all of his life this pact of peace."

Again the murmur ran through the crowd. Matteo, his eyes shining with the wonder of it, cried eagerly, "We promise to feed him always and to keep our part of the pact! Do we not?" he added, turning to the people. And their shout in answer rang back from the mountainside. The wolf stirred uneasily, and Francis lifted the lean head in his hand and looked deep into the puzzled eyes.

"Brother Wolf," he said, "as you have pledged your word to me outside of the city to keep and preserve your promise, I desire that here again before the people of Gubbio you shall renew that pledge, and promise that you will never play me false in the surety that I have given for you."

He dropped the wolf's head and moved a pace away. A breath of doubt swept through the crowd. But Francis' face did not change. For a long moment the wolf hesitated. Then he rose and, taking one step toward Francis, he lifted the gray paw again and laid it in his hand.

At that the tension broke, and joy and wonder and relief swept through the people as a wind sweeps through a field of wheat. A woman on the outskirts of the crowd ran to her home near by and came back with a great copper pot filled with rice and gravy and vegetables which she had prepared for the evening meal. Fearlessly she went to the wolf and put it down in front of him. For an instant he sniffed it suspiciously; then his head disappeared in the pot and they could hear the eager lapping of his tongue. When he had finished every grain and licked the pot to cleanness again, he looked up into the woman's face, and—"*Mille grazie, Signora,*" his eyes said. In the crowd a child laughed and clapped his hands.

And from that day the Wolf of Gubbio walked its streets as freely as one of the citizens. Every evening, winter and summer, he called at a house door, and the housewives vied with one another in preparing properly his evening meal. The children played with him, and often in the sunny noons of spring and autumn he lay stretched like a great dog in the square before the fountain. Strangers, seeing him, would wonder and perhaps be frightened. But the citizens would laugh at their fears. They would say proudly, "He will not hurt you. He is *our* wolf—the Wolf of Gubbio." When, after two peaceful years, he died of old age, they buried him in the garden of the convent. There, year after year, the oleanders shook out their white and crimson blossoms above him and the cypress trees stood like tall, dark candles beside him.

Today the citizens of Gubbio point proudly to a fresco that is painted in soft, pale colors on the walls of their great Palazzo dei Consoli. There is the little square with the fountain, exactly as it was seven hundred years ago. There are the awed and wondering people—the men and the women and the children. There is St. Francis in his brown robe, and there beside him, his head bowed under the saint's gentle hand, stands the Wolf of Gubbio.

The Peddler of Ballaghadereen

⚬ℂ *Ruth Sawyer* ℂ⚬

There was once a peddler who lived long ago at the crossroads in Ballaghadereen, in the County of Mayo. He lived by himself in a bit of a cabin with one room to it; and that so small that a man could stand in the middle of the floor and without taking a step, he could lift the latch on the front door, he could lift the latch on the back door, and he could hang the kettle over the turf. That is how small and snug it was.

Outside the cabin the peddler had a bit of a garden. In it he planted carrots and cabbages, onions, and potatoes. In the center grew a cherry tree—as brave and fine a tree as you would find anywhere in Ireland. Every spring it flowered, the white blossoms covering it like a fresh falling of snow. Every summer it bore cherries as red as heart's blood.

But every year, after the garden was planted the wee brown hares would come from the copse nearby and nibble-nibble here, and nibble-nibble there, until there was not a thing left, barely, to grow into a full-sized vegetable that a man could harvest for his table. And every summer as the cherries began to ripen, the blackbirds came in whirling flocks and ate the cherries as fast as they ripened.

The neighbors that lived thereabouts minded this and nodded their heads and said: "Master Peddler—you're a poor, simple man, entirely. You let the wild creatures thieve from you without lifting your hand to stop them."

And the peddler would always nod his head back at them and laugh and answer: "Nay, then, 'tis not thieving they are at all. They pay well for what they take. Look you—on yonder cherry tree the blackbirds sing sweeter nor they sing on any cherry tree in Ballaghadereen. And the brown hares make good company at dusk-hour for a lonely man."

In the country round-about, every day when there was market, a wedding, or a fair, the peddler would be off at ring-o'-day, his pack strapped on his back, one foot ahead of the other, fetching him along the road. And when he reached the town diamond he would open his pack, spread it on the green turf; and making a hollow of his two hands he would call:

"Come buy a trinket—come buy a brooch—
Come buy a kerchief of scarlet or yellow!"

In no time at all there would be a great crowding of lads and lasses and children about him, searching his pack for what they might be wanting. And like as not some barefooted lad would hold up a jack-knife and ask: "How much for this, Master Peddler?"

And the peddler would answer, "Half a crown."

And the lad would put it back, shaking his head dolefully.

"Faith, I haven't the half of that, nor likely ever to have it."

And the Peddler would pull the lad over to him and whisper in his ear: "Bother the half crown. Take the knife—'twill rest a deal more easy in your pocket than in my pack."

Then, like as not, some lass would hold up a blue kerchief to her yellow curls and ask: "Master Peddler, what is the price of this?"

And the peddler would answer: "One shilling, sixpence."

And the lass would put it back, the smile gone from her face, and she turning away.

And the peddler would catch up the kerchief again and tie it himself about her curls and laugh and say: "Faith, there it looks far prettier than ever it looks in my pack. Take it, with God's blessing."

So it would go—a brooch to this one and a top to that. There were days when the peddler took in little more than a few farthings. But after those days he would sing his way homeward; and the shrewd ones would watch him passing by and wag their fingers at him and say: "You're a poor, simple man, Master Peddler. You'll never be putting a penny by for your old age. You'll end your days like the blackbirds, whistling for crumbs at our back doors. Why, even the vagabond dogs know they can wheedle the half of the bread you are carrying in your pouch, you're that simple."

Which likewise was true. Every stray, hungry dog knew him the length and breadth of the county. Rarely did he follow a road without one tagging his heels, sure of a noon-day sharing of bread and cheese.

There were days when he went abroad without his pack, when there was no market day, no wedding or fair. These he spent with the children, who would have followed him about like the dogs, had their mothers let them. On these days he would sit himself down on some doorstep and when a crowd of children had gathered he would tell them tales—old tales of Ireland—tales of the good folk, of the heroes, of the saints. He knew them all, and he knew how to tell them, the way the children would never be forgetting one of them, but carry them in their hearts until they were old.

And whenever he finished a tale he would say, like as not, laughing and pinching the cheek of some wee lass: "Mind well your manners, whether you are at home or abroad, for you can never be telling what good folk, or saint or hero you may be fetching up with on the road—or who may come knocking at your doors. Aye, when Dermuid, or Fionn or Oisin or Saint Patrick walked the earth they were poor and simple and plain men; it took death to put a grand memory on them. And the poor and the simple and the old today may be heroes tomorrow—you never can be telling. So keep a kind word for all, and a gentling hand."

Often an older would stop to listen to the scraps of words he was saying; and often as not he would go his way, wagging his finger and mumbling: "The poor, simple man. He's as foolish as the blackbirds."

Spring followed winter in Ireland; and summer followed close upon the heels of both. And winter came again and the peddler grew old. His pack grew lighter and lighter, until the neighbors could hear the trinkets jangling inside as he passed, so little was left inside. They would nod their heads and say to one another: "Like as not his pockets are growing as empty as his pack. Time will come, with winter at hand, when he will be at our back doors, begging crumbs, along with the blackbirds."

The time did come, as the neighbors had prophesied it would, smug and proper, when the peddler's pack was empty. When he had naught in his pockets and naught in his dresser cupboard, and he went hungry to bed. Now it is more than likely that hungry men will dream; and the peddler of Ballaghadereen had a strange dream that night.

He dreamed that there came a sound of knocking in the middle of the night. Then the latch on the front door lifted, the door opened without a creak or a cringe, and inside the cabin stepped Saint Patrick. Standing in the open doorway the good man pointed a finger down the road and across Mayo County to the city of Dublin; and he spoke in a voice tuned as low as the wind over the bogs: "Peddler, peddler of Ballaghadereen, take *that* road on the morrow. When you get to the bridge that spans the Liffey stand where you are and you will hear what you were meant to hear."

In the morning the peddler awoke and remembered the dream. He rubbed his stomach and found it mortal empty; he stood on his legs and found them trembling under him; and he said to himself: "Faith, an empty stomach and weak legs are the worst traveling companions a man can have, and Dublin is a long way off. I'll bide where I am."

That night the peddler went hungrier to bed, and again came the dream. There came the knocking on the door, the lifting of the latch. The door opened and Saint Patrick stood there, pointing the road to Dublin and saying: "Peddler, peddler of Ballaghadereen, take *that* road on the morrow. When you get to the bridge that spans the Liffey stand where you are and you will hear what you were meant to hear!"

The second day it was the same as the first. The peddler felt the hunger and the weakness stronger in him, and stayed where he was. But when he woke after the third night and the third coming of the dream, he rose and strapped his pack from long habit upon his back and took the road to Dublin. For three long weary days he traveled, barely staying his fast, and on the fourth day he came into the city.

Early in the day he found the bridge spanning the river and all the lee long day he stood there, changing his weight from one foot to the other, shifting his pack to ease the drag of it, scanning the faces of all who passed by. But although a great tide of people swept this way, and a great tide swept that, no one stopped and spoke to him.

At the end of the day he felt that the world and life itself had ended for him.

"I'll find me a blind alley," he thought, "and like an old dog I'll lay me down in it and die." Slowly he moved off the bridge, slowly he moved along the narrow walk going somewhere—anywhere. As he passed across from the Head Inn of Dublin, the door opened and out came the landlord.

To the peddler's astonishment he crossed the thoroughfare and hurried after him. He clapped a strong hand on his shoulder and cried: "Arra, man, hold a minute! All day I've been watching you. All day I have seen you standing on the bridge like an old rook with rent wings. And of all the people passing from the west to the east, and of all the people passing from the east to the west, not one crossing over the bridge spoke with you. Now I am filled with a great curiosity entirely to know what fetched you here."

Seeing hunger and weariness on the peddler he drew him towards the Inn. "Come, in return for having my curiosity satisfied you shall have rest in the kitchen yonder, with bread and cheese and ale. Come."

So the peddler rested his bones by the kitchen hearth and he ate as he hadn't eaten in many days. He was satisfied at long last and the landlord plied his question a second time. "Tell me, peddler, what fetched you here?"

"For three nights running I had a dream—" began the peddler, but he got no further.

The landlord of the Head Inn threw back his head and laughed. How he laughed, rocking on his feet, shaking the whole length of him.

"A dream you had, by my soul, a dream!" He spoke when he could get his breath. "I could be telling you were the cut of a man to have dreams, and to listen to them, what's more. Rags on your back and hunger in your cheeks and age upon you, and I'll wager not a farthing in your pouch. Well, God's blessing on you and your dreams."

The peddler got to his feet, saddled his pack and made for the door. He had one foot over the sill when the landlord hurried after him and again clapped a hand on his shoulder.

"Hold, Master Peddler," he said, "I too had a dream, three nights running." He burst into laughter again, remembering it. "I dreamed there came a knocking on this very door, and the latch lifted and, standing in the doorway, as you are standing this minute, I saw Saint Patrick. He pointed with one finger to the road running westward and he said: 'Landlord, Landlord of the Head Inn, take *that* road to a place called Ballaghadereen. When you come to the crossroads you will find a wee cabin, and beside the cabin a wee garden, and in the center of the garden a cherry tree. Dig deep under the tree and you will find gold—much gold.' "

The landlord paused and drew his sleeve across his mouth to hush his laughter.

"A place called Ballaghadereen—I never heard of it! Gold under a cherry tree—whoever heard of gold under a cherry tree! There is only one dream that I hear, waking or sleeping, and it's the dream of gold, much gold, in my own pocket. Aye, listen, 'tis a good dream." And the landlord thrust a hand into his pouch and jangled the coins loudly in the peddler's ear.

Back to Ballaghadereen went the peddler, one foot ahead of the other. How he got there I cannot be telling you. He unslung his pack, took up a mattock lying nearby, and dug under the cherry tree. He dug deep and felt at last the scraping of the mattock against something hard and smooth. It took him time to uncover it and he found it to be an old sea chest, of foreign pattern and workmanship, bound around with bands of brass. These he broke, and lifting the lid he found the chest full of gold, tarnished and clotted with mold; pieces-of-six and pieces-of-eight and Spanish doubloons.

I cannot begin to tell the half of the goodness and the kindness that the peddler put into the spending of that gold. But this I know. He built a chapel at the crossroads—a resting place for all weary travelers, journeying thither. And for all who came upon that road the peddler had a welcome and food, so long as he lived.

And after he had gone, the children, who had grown to be his neighbors, had a statue made of him and placed it facing the crossroads, that it might seem as if he were still welcoming all who came that way. And should you go to Ballaghadereen today you would find the peddler there, like as not, with pack on his back, a dog at his heels, and a welcome for you.

Henry's Lincoln

❀⟦ *Louise A. Neyhart* ⟧❀

Henry opened his eyes to the early morning and began fitting little songs to the sounds which came through the open window of his tiny bedroom. To the clink-clank of the pump he hummed the words:

"Today's the day, today's the day,
no time to dawdle on the way!"

He knew as soon as the pump stopped his mother would call, "Henry, Henry," and that he would answer drowsily, "Yes, Ma," and roll over to wait until she came to the stairs with her more vigorous call: "Henree!"

But this morning he didn't wait. He jumped out of the bed and stumbled to the window. His father's lantern was bobbing and zig-zagging towards the barn.

He dressed quickly and was downstairs in a jiffy.

"Morning, Ma," he called as he splashed his face with water.

"Land sakes, Henry! You awake and here already? I didn't call you but once this morning. What's ailing you, child?"

"Have to milk the pigs and feed the cows, Ma."

"Henry, what are you saying?" Mrs. Oaks laughed, stirring the batter. "You're all mixed up."

"Milk the cows, I mean, and . . ." he corrected himself as he dashed outside and away to the barn.

It was a quiet August morning. The cows rustling in their stalls, the grunting hogs, and the pigeons cooing in the barn loft broke the stillness. In the distance there was a friendly call of quail. Henry took a deep breath. It was good to smell the sweet clover and the fresh hay. Deep inside he felt there never would be another day like this.

"Morning, Pa." Henry gave the cow a shove as he planted his stool and bucket. "Over Bess, over Bess."

Mr. Oaks peered over the top of his glasses, saying, "Pretty spry this morning, Son, and no school today, either."

"We want to get to Freeport before everything starts, don't we, Pa?"

"Freeport? Oh, oh, yes, this *is* the day of the big doings, sure enough. Guess it's going to be a big battle all right, with plenty of shooting on both sides."

"Real shooting, Pa?" Henry stopped his milking a moment in surprise. His teacher, Mr. Barnes, hadn't said anything about shooting when he had announced a special school holiday to go to the Great Debate.

Then Old Bess swished her tail in Henry's face and brought him to his senses. "I know; a debate's like a battle, you mean, Pa?"

"Yep."

"But with words for bullets?"

"Yep."

"And instead of two armies there'll be two men, fighting each other with big arguments."

"Yep, that's right, Son. Fiery arguments instead of firearms. Sort of a duel, I guess. A duel between the Little Giant and the Tall Sucker." Mr. Oaks laughed. "It's going to be great, all right."

Henry, lost in thought for a moment, went back to his milking, telling himself he must not waste any more time. Freeport was no small trip from the farm.

"Who are you going to be for, Pa?" he asked eagerly, "Douglas or Lincoln?" Up in his room Henry had a Senator Douglas badge, and he was counting on wearing it, for Douglas was the Little Giant.

Mr. Oaks thought a while. "I wouldn't say right off," he answered, "not until I know what they've *both* got to say. That's just why they're debating: so folks can see and hear them standing up to each other, arguing it out face to face. That way we can find out which one is the best man for us."

"The best man, Pa!" Henry said. "Stephen Arnold Douglas is the most famous U. S. Senator we've ever had from Illinois. And now this new man Lincoln wants to be Senator instead of him."

"Say, you know how to argufy too, Henry," Mr. Oaks exclaimed. "Let's hear what you've go to say and we'll have a little debate right here by ourselves."

"Well, what I say is, Pa," Henry went on, "Mr. Lincoln, he's never been a Senator before."

"So why not give him a chance too?"

"But you said, Pa, we should have the best man. How'll we know just by listening to him talk if he'll be any better than the one we already have?"

"By finding out what he believes in, Henry."

This reply made Henry thoughtful. "Gee," he said, "That's what I like now: to hear folks tell what they believe in."

"That's a sign you're growing up, Son," the father observed quietly.

The two became silent. The milk fell with a strumming sound into the two wooden pails.

"People will be coming to Freeport from miles around," Mr. Oaks reflected. "More folks than a fly-hatch down here on the creek."

"Let's hurry, Pa," Henry urged.

Mr. Oaks shook his head. "Much as your Ma and I would like to go, we just can't with all the work here."

"Oh, Pa!" Henry exclaimed. He didn't know how he could bear this disappointment. Here he had counted upon so many things: wearing his badge at the Big Debate, and seeing the famous Senator in person instead of just in pictures. "Senator Douglas might never come out our way again," he pleaded.

"Look at those windrows of hay out in the field, Son," Mr. Oaks said, "and then look up in the sky at those big clouds. What does that mean?"

"Means it might rain, and so we got to get the hay in," Henry admitted reluctantly. Hay was very important, he knew, for if it got spoiled by the rain, the cows and the horses wouldn't have enough to eat this winter. Especially his favorite horse Prince. Folks said Prince was the handsomest, spryest horse in all northern Illinois. Henry figured he'd rather go without anything himself than see Prince go without hay.

"We farmers," Mr. Oaks said quietly, "have to know how to take the tough along with the good."

"Yep, I guess we do, Pa."

Mr. Oaks finished milking his cow and stood up. "But we also got our duty to do as citizens. Somebody in this family ought to go to that debate, don't you think?"

Henry wondered what was coming.

"*You* go, Henry," his father said, rumpling the boy's hair, "and mind you get everything into that touseled head of yours, so you can tell your Ma and Pa all about it."

Henry's face brightened. "Alone? You mean . . . to go to Freeport . . . all alone?" The words seemed to stick in his throat.

"Sure thing. A boy has to go to town alone some day. It might as well be today."

"Oh, Pa!" Henry jumped up from his milking stool. "Can I drive Prince?"

"Why, of course. I don't know any other man I'd rather trust him with."

Henry's heart went flippity-flop, flippity-flop.

He and his father finished the chores and started back to the house for breakfast. When they got near they could smell corn-meal mush frying and maple sirup boiling. Mrs. Oaks' kitchen always had the best smells. Catsup and plum butter in the big preserving kettle, and potatoes sizzling gently in the iron skillet were the smells Henry liked best.

"Ma," Henry shouted, hurrying into the house, "I'm going, I'm going!"

Mr. Oaks washed in the tin basin and dried on the roller towel. "Yes sir-ree, Sarah," he said, "our boy's going to the Lincoln-Douglas Debate up at Freeport."

"I did so hope we could all go," Mrs. Oaks said wistfully.

"Never you mind, Ma, I'll tell you everything about it, honest injun!"

Mrs. Oaks smiled proudly at her son, and said, "All right, Henry, you be our representative!"

There was no time to waste. Henry carried chunks of wood and chucked them into the woodbox by the stove. He fed and watered the chickens; then he rushed to fill the buckets at the pump.

"Now let me see your ears—mind you scrub your neck, too," Mrs. Oaks said, "and don't just wipe all the dirt on the towel—SCRUB! I'll pack you a lunch to take along."

Henry swished the soap suds around the basin and ducked his face into the bubbles. He took particular pains so there would be no streaks. He changed into his new homespun suit his mother had made for him, and took care to change the Douglas badge to his best jacket. He polished his shoes until they shone like the new stovepipe in the parlor.

"Would you have any use for a few coppers?" Mr. Oaks asked, as he reached into the majolica sugar bowl in the cupboard.

"Coppers!" Henry exclaimed, counting the bright new pennies: "One, two, three, four, five, six, seven, eight, nine, ten." They were all his. "Gee, thanks!" he said, and slid them into his pocket. "It will be fine to have money in my pocket, just like you, Pa, when you go to town." Henry liked to touch the pennies and make them jingle.

"Come and eat your mush, Henry," his mother called. "It's all ready."

Henry ate his breakfast quickly, snatched his lunch box, and ran to the barn. He led Prince, the spirited white horse, from the stall and hitched him to the old buggy.

He put two flags on Prince's head. "Now you look like a circus horse," Henry told him. Prince seemed to know this was a special occasion and was anxious to be off.

"Giddap, Prince," Henry shouted. He lifted the reins and waved good-bye to his mother and father, who stood watching in the doorway, until he was out of sight.

Henry knew how much his father and mother would like to be along instead of working at home, and missing all he was going to see. He was a little sad about that, but he felt better when he thought about how he would bring it all home to them.

For a long time he had dreamed of this first trip to town all by himself. Now at last he was going!

He looked up at the sky. It was a soft blue like the delphiniums that grew in his mother's garden; for the heavy dark clouds had vanished and white billowy clouds like feather beds floated about.

"Today's the day. . . ." Again the little song he had sung to himself upon waking this morning came into his mind. "Today's—the twenty-seventh of August." In the kitchen at home hung a calendar, and he remembered having glanced at the date. "August 27, 1858. That's the date of the Great Debate," he said to himself, making a rhyme of it.

It was Friday today and he was driving right past his school. This was a one-room log cabin. Only yesterday there had been a fight between Aaron Hart and Rufus Spence. Aaron was for Douglas and Rufus for Lincoln. They called each other names, then fists began to fly, and the boys were rolling in the dust by the time the teacher came out to stop them. Aaron had a black eye and Rufus a bloody nose.

"Boys, these are trying times in politics," Mr. Barnes had said, "and every young American should be wide awake to differences of opinion. But no more fisticuffs! Tomorrow you are going to the Debate, I hope, and there you will see the grown-up American way to fight out a political argument. Shake hands!"

Now, on his way to the Debate, Henry wondered what it would be like. Would the two men talk back and forth to each other, cutting in and interrupting? How were they going to do it?

To get there sooner he decided to leave the easy, everyday road that skirted the woods and to take the road that went straight through the timber. He pulled the reins, and Prince turned into the dimly cut wagon tracks. This road was shorter but it was rougher than the other, and a bit scary. The large tree trunks and heavy foliage of the giant oaks, elms, and maples made it seem dark. But Prince was the same white as in the bright cloud up in the sky and he seemed to light up the shadowy forest as he led the way through.

Wild turkeys, squirrels, rabbits, and chipmunks were darting through the wild grapevines that hung from the bushes and trees. Many a time Henry had seen snakes and even rattlers in these woods.

Just a few weeks before he had killed a bobcat in the very elm tree he was now passing. He had shot it with a bow and arrow which his Indian friend, Owasah, had made for him. He remembered how he had trembled when he first saw the cold, yellow eyes of this treacherous animal. And how his heart had pounded when he drew his arrow. For if it didn't find its mark, the bobcat would leap at him, with tearing claws. And today he wouldn't be riding to the Debate! Now he was proudly wearing the cap Owasah had made for him out of the bobcat skin.

That had been a duel all right, between a boy and a beast, Henry reflected, and he had won.

He and Prince were out of the woods by now, going at a good clip on the flat road.

Suddenly there was a shrill whistle. Prince perked up his ears, and switched his tail uneasily. Henry knew it was the ten o'clock train from Dixon. The train came closer and closer; the big black engine was pulling hard, chugging up the slight incline with a full head of steam. Prince shied to the side of the road, then reared up on his hind feet and pranced about, doing a jig.

Henry stood up. He pulled the reins with all his strength, saying, "Easy now, easy, Prince, nothing will hurt you!"

With one eye on Prince and the other eye on the train, Henry could see cars crowded with people, going to the Debate. On the rear platform of the last coach stood a tall, strange-looking man, who waved and shouted, "Good driving, young fellow, good driving!"

Henry watched the train until, in a few moments, only the smoke remained in the distance.

Prince settled down to his natural trot, greatly relieved that the big, black, puffing monster was gone.

After crossing the covered bridge, Henry found old Grandpa Higgins sitting by the side of the road. His head was bowed over his long, white beard. Holding his hickory stick with both hands, he looked very tired.

"Whoa, Prince!" Henry called, "Going to the Debate, Grandpa?"

"Wouldn't miss it for all the mud in the river! Just stopped to rest a mite. By jingo, I ain't as spry as I used to be." Grandpa Higgins chuckled, "My feet don't work so good, but my head still works. Ain't full of a lot of durned foolishness." He groaned as he climbed unsteadily into the buggy. "That's the trouble with most folks: don't use their heads enough."

"Yep," Henry said, moving over to make room for Grandpa. He snapped the reins and Prince went right into a trot.

Grandpa cleared his throat and said, "Well, here you're doing your own driving to town, Henry. Seems just yesterday you were only a little tad!"

"Yep." Henry looked proudly around the countryside. Goldenrod and wild asters made it look like a quilt of yellow and purple calico.

"Ain't your Ma and Pa going?" Grandpa asked.

"They're making hay, but I'm going to tell them all about it."

"Well, you'll have to pay right good attention then. Talk'll be nip and tuck between those two." Grandpa paused a moment, glancing at Henry's badge. "Humph! See you're a Douglas man." Then, with a twinkle in his eye, he added, "Maybe I better get down and walk. I'm for Abe Lincoln myself."

Henry laughed. Grandpa could be for Lincoln till kingdom come and still be welcome to ride.

"Would you like some of my lunch, Grandpa Higgins?" Henry said, remembering there were *two* fried ham sandwiches as well as a good large square of gingerbread in it.

"Smells right good. Don't mind if I do," Grandpa said. "Nothing I like better than a ham sandwich and a piece of gingerbread to top it off. But I don't want to rob you?"

"No robbing, Grandpa; there's plenty."

"Thank you, Henry."

Grandpa looked thoughtful as he chewed for a while. Then he said, "So you reckon the Little Giant is going to chaw up Old Abe, eh?"

"Don't know, Grandpa. I've heard folks say Mr. Lincoln can argue down any man alive," Henry admitted.

"Sure he can, just about. I like Lincoln. He used to be a farmer like your father and me, but he studied hard and made himself a lawyer. He's a right smart man, I tell you, and honest too."

"Senator Douglas used to be a farmer once, too," Henry replied, "but after that he was a judge. And look how long he's been United States Senator for our state of Illinois. He's a great man."

"Look here, Son, Abe Lincoln may not be famous all over the world, like Douglas, but he's against slavery. He split his own logs to build his fences instead of owning black slaves to do it for him. How would you like to be bought and sold and made to work and never get paid for it, and get horsewhipped if you didn't work hard enough?"

"I wouldn't like that."

"And all because you happened to be born with a different color of skin?" Grandpa continued. "I saw a slave market once. There were signs all over offering to pay the highest prices in cash for Negroes: sort of a livery stable for buying and selling humans, it was. Say, now, you were a colored boy, just getting to be a man, big enough now to go to town and be a little your own boss. Know what they'd do with you? They'd auction you off like a young colt, take you away from your mother and father, far off where you'd never see them again."

Grandpa spoke in low tones of deep anger, as if all this had been done to him or to someone he knew very well.

"Why, you know, Henry, you treat your horse here better than they treat a lot of those poor slave-folks." Grandpa squinted his eyes in serious thought. "All you got to ask yourself while listening to that there debate this afternoon is: is a colored person just a kind of property you own, like a cow or horse or dog? Or is he a human being, just as much as you and I are?"

"I never thought about it just like that, Grandpa," Henry said.

He glanced down at his badge. "But I don't think that Senator Douglas would be for anything so cruel, do you?"

All at once a loud boom seemed to shake the earth, and Prince bolted in fright. Henry looked up in the sky to see where the thundercloud might be as he got Prince under control.

"Cannons," Grandpa said.

"Cannons? You mean they're doing *real* shooting?"

"Sure, it's real. It's a real salute to Old Abe. Guess his train's just arrived."

"Giddap, giddap, Prince, or we'll be late!" Henry yelled. It seemed much farther to town today than ever before.

"Guess you didn't hear the firing when your man got in last night," Grandpa said. "Douglas's train carries a flat-car, and he has two brass cannons mounted on it that are fired at every place the train stops."

Prince was striding very fast now as if he liked the cool air. The wind brought faint sounds of music.

Down the street were brass bands playing, glittering in the sun like the music they made. Everywhere were flags and banners. The streets were gaily decorated with red-white-and-blue streamers. Here and there volleys of cheering arose. Henry wanted to stand up and shout.

"Look!" He cried. "We're here!"

They were only at the edge of town, though. Henry and Grandpa agreed it would be better to find a hitching place for Prince right now. After watering the horse at a trough, Henry tied him. "I'll be back, Prince," he said, giving him a lump of sugar from his pocket, and stroking his soft nose.

Here on the outskirts, families sat around eating lunches they had brought from home. Melons, cakes, cold chicken. It was like a big picnic.

"Never's been so many people in Freeport all at once," Grandpa said as he shook his head in amazement. "Makes you wonder where they all come from."

Fields and hillsides were crowded with campers, who surrounded the city like an invading army. From all directions they came to hear the Great Debate: over long weary miles of hot and dusty prairie. Some on foot, some on horseback, others in prairie schooners and hay wagons, and still others in trains. There was even a special train from Chicago.

"I expect they come from every county in northern Illinois and down from Wisconsin too," Grandpa said. "Well, so long, Henry. I'll meet you after the Debate."

Henry hurried to get into the milling mob of people in the train part of the town.

On one corner a Douglas brass band was playing against a Lincoln brass band. Each had its own song, and was trying to drown the other out.

Every place he looked were peddlers barking in outlandish voices to sell their wares: flags, badges, lemonade, pain-killers, and medicine to make hair grow on bald heads. "Tell your fortune, mister? Ten cents," a Gypsy woman called. Henry held on to his ten coppers.

Men were talking, joking, laughing, and some were arguing, their faces red and their eyes flashing. Clumps of people formed wherever an argument was going on.

"Nonsense! Douglas doesn't say he's for slavery," Henry heard somebody say, and he thought he'd stop and listen to this argument. A tall man in a linen duster was holding forth. "All Douglas says is if we don't quit quarreling over the question we'll get to throwing things around and wreck the whole nation. That's just common sense."

"But, sir, we can't avoid the question," said a man with a high collar and a blue silk scarf wrapped tightly around it. "A new State like Kansas wants to come into the Union. After her there will be other States. And you think they should be allowed to come in as slave States?"

"Allowed?" the other man bellowed. "Who does the allowing in this country, if not the people themselves! If the people of Kansas vote for slavery, that's *their* business. Not ours."

"Sure, that's the point," a man in a fancy vest and long coat tails put in. "Here in Illinois we don't think slavery's right. But we should mind our own business, not tell the other States what to do. I'm for little Doug."

"Hi, Henry!" someone called.

It was Aaron Hart, who also was for Douglas. His black eye seemed bigger than the day before. "Come on," he said, "the parade's coming!"

People were pushing and crowding along the curbs to see it.

First came the brass band. The bandsmen were very splendid in long blue coats with bright gold buttons down the front. The music was so big and wonderful that your feet wanted to get right in and march with it. Henry and Aaron couldn't march with the band, but they did the next best thing. They ran along beside it for a ways, dodging in and out of the crowd.

Then came a squad of soldiers with the Stars and Stripes. It was the most beautiful and largest American flag Henry had ever seen. It had a gold fringe, and it tossed in the wind as though on the swell of the grand music around it. Men took off their hats. Little chills ran down Henry's back. He and Aaron took off their hats too.

Then the mayor and city officials rode by in buggies decorated with flowers and small flags.

Ladies waved handkerchiefs from hallways and upstairs windows. Henry wished his mother and father could be here to see all this. So he watched it for all he was worth to be sure of remembering every bit of it.

Marchers came by, bearing big banners with slogans on them:

"ABE THE GIANT KILLER"

"THE LITTLE GIANT FOR US"

Most astonishing of all the things in the parade was a very long wagon drawn by sixteen pairs of oxen and managed by three drivers with whips. At times it sounded as if a musket regiment were cracking those whips. And on the wagon were several men with mauls, wedges, and axes. They were splitting large logs into rails. A cotton banner proclaimed:

"WE WANT THE RAILSPLITTER"

Henry and Aaron got in line and marched with the parade until they came to the court house. At the court house square, people were having a big barbecue.

"Those sandwiches smell good. Let's get one," Henry suggested.

"Sure—they don't cost anything, and I'm hungry," Aaron said.

Three beeves were being roasted over a big ditch. Ladies in bonnets and big aprons were serving the free sandwiches.

Henry and Aaron squeezed into the long line to wait their turn. After they got up to the tables and were served, Aaron ran off with his sandwich to some cousins of his he saw across the square.

"Henry Oaks, you dear boy!" a high voice exclaimed. It was Miss Martha, who sang in the church choir. "Henry, I've just come from the Brewster House," Miss Martha went on, bubbling with excitement. "The street in front of the hotel was black with people, shouting for both the men. And what do you think? They came out on the balcony—yes, they did. Mr. Douglas and Mr. Lincoln came out together arm in arm, and bowed again and again."

"Gee wilikers, I'm going to get down there," Henry said and abruptly dashed away, gobbling the sandwich as he ran.

The Brewster House stood majestically on the corner of the

main street. It was a new four-story hotel with a balcony around the second floor. Henry looked up at the tall building. A flag swirled in the breeze on the top. He wondered if he dare go into the hotel alone. Surely there would be much to see inside—and he did want to see everything.

Henry stood in the doorway shyly. Groups of men were standing around talking excitedly. Brass spittoons glistened like gold. There were big, comfortable chairs, and soft carpets.

In the far corner of the room was a counter with a sign "Pink Lemonade ten cents," and there, right in front of the sign was Rufus, drinking pink lemonade. Henry felt much bolder, now that he saw a familiar face. He crossed the room and slapped Rufus on the shoulder.

"What're you doing here?"

Rufus was so startled he almost spilled the precious lemonade. "Came here with my uncle," Rufus gulped. "He's in a parlor upstairs right now, talking business with Mr. Lincoln. Mmmm, want a sip of my lemonade? It's the best I ever tasted."

"Thanks, I'm going to buy some for myself—I've got money!" Henry said proudly. Ten cents seemed a lot to spend for a lemonade, when he could buy it for five cents at a stand on the street, but this was pink lemonade, and it was worth something to stand in the luxurious Brewster House to drink it. "I'll have a pink lemonade," he said to the clerk importantly, as he counted the ten broad coppers and placed them on the counter.

It was a drink fit for a king. Henry licked his lips and wiped his mouth on his sleeve when he had drained the last drops from the glass.

"Want to see something?" Rufus whispered.

"Sure—what?"

"Come on, I'll show you." Rufus looked around to see if anyone was watching.

Henry followed Rufus down the long hall to a hat shelf. There were hats and more hats—there were hats of every description. Rufus pointed to a broad-brimmed silk hat. "That belongs to Senator Douglas!"

"It does?" Henry gazed in awe at the sumptuous gray silk hat. The hat of a United States Senator, he told himself.

"Douglas is your man, isn't he?" Rufus asked slyly.

"I'm not saying!"

"You're wearing his badge," Rufus insisted.

"Yeh, but I guess you ought to hear what a man's got to say, before you say you're for him."

"Dare you to put on the Senator's hat, Henry."

"Is anybody looking?"

"Nah—go on."

The broad-brimmed hat came down over Henry's ears. "Monstrous big, ain't it?" Henry said.

"But look at *this* hat!" Rufus said proudly. "This belongs to Abraham Lincoln. I'm for him, and no ifs nor ands about it. Dare you to try this one on, too!"

It was a tall, shabby black cloth hat.

Henry put on the hat. It rested on his ears.

"It almost fits you, Henry!"

Assuming great dignity, Henry straightened his shoulders, and tipped the hat gallantly to Rufus.

Rufus had to cover his mouth with his hand to keep from laughing out loud.

Then Rufus put on the Senator's hat. Henry and Rufus looked at each other very seriously, each trying to make believe he was the illustrious man who owned the hat. They lifted the hats and bowed to each other most solemnly.

A burst of laughter came to the ears of the boys. They turned and saw several gentlemen. Foremost among them was a sturdy little man with a large round head that seemed almost too big for him.

At once the boys recognized him from his many pictures. It was Senator Stephen Arnold Douglas!

But his large stern face was smiling. His wavy hair and the ruffle of his elegant shirt seemed a part of that smile.

Amid the clatter of laughter a voice from behind the Senator exclaimed, "A Lincoln badge under the Douglas hat, and a Douglas badge under the Lincoln hat!"

Quickly the boys returned the hats to the shelf.

"Boys," the Senator chortled at their sides, "let me shake your hands."

It was a good strong handshake, Henry thought: you could feel the solid man behind it. No wonder they called him The Little Giant!

"Almost time for us to be there," somebody said. "Is the Senator's carriage waiting outside?"

"We will walk," the Senator said decisively. He sounded and looked like a statesman all right. A wide mouth and a big oratorical voice. The kind that made laws, Henry was thinking.

A large group of men moved off with the Senator, out of the hotel, while the boys, still in a daze, trailed behind.

A white-haired man dressed in Sunday broadcloth said to another, "It would have been a splendid sight to see him riding to the grove in that beautiful carriage drawn by those two fine dapple grays of his. But I suppose that wouldn't have gone so well today with those farm people. They'd think he was putting on airs."

"Especially when they see how the Lincoln outfit is bringing *him* to the Debate," said the other man.

"Let's wait and go there with Mr. Lincoln," Rufus said.

But Henry wished to stick with the Douglas crowd as it streamed down the street amid cheering Hip-hip-hoora-ays!

So lively was the throng that Rufus went along with it at Henry's side.

It was glorious fun marching in all this noise and color, even though the air was chilly and darkening for rain. Bright little flags everywhere. Men waving their hats. Ladies' handkerchiefs fluttering. Henry forgot about the slaves. Who would think that all this uproarious glee had anything to do with slavery?

Then Henry saw Jim Ludds standing with his little boy and girl, Mose and Becky. They were colored folks and all three were wearing Lincoln badges. Each had a small flag, and instead of waving it as the Douglas people trooped by, Jim, Mose and Becky held their little flags as high in the air as they could—the way Henry's mother would sometimes hold up a candle to see better in a dark room.

This gave Henry a deep sort of sorry feeling inside. He didn't want to see the Ludds owned as slaves. Not even by the nicest owners who might be just as kind to them as he was to Prince. For the Ludds were people, not beasts. "This flag will keep us from being slaves," they seemed to say. "It will not let you put any more slave states into this Union."

As Henry and Rufus neared the grounds, the crowd got louder and louder.

"Hurrah for Douglas!"

The grounds, a grove not far from the hotel, were quite open timber. Most of the trees were young and not very big. The platform was about three feet high. Around it were plank seats for people to sit on.

Some boys were climbing trees to see, but Henry and Rufus thought they would rather be closer to the speakers. They wedged their way to the front row.

Eliza Simms, from school, and her father were sitting in one of the front rows, right in front of the platform. Eliza smiled shyly, and smoothed her full, pink skirt. Freckles and golden hair, drawn tightly, peeked from her blue bonnet.

"Can we sit here with you, Eliza?" Henry asked.

"I'll ask Pa to move over," she said.

Mr. Simms shoved and the fat woman on the other side of Eliza pushed, and Henry and Rufus squeezed in.

"Eliza's your girl!" Rufus whispered slyly to Henry.

"I'm not saying."

"You toted her books home last night."

"Maybe I did."

"Well, that makes her your girl," Rufus said conclusively.

By this time the committee almost had to fight to clear a way for the speakers. The people were cheering and shouting. Senator Douglas, smiling and bowing with much self-assurance, stepped to the platform.

"Stephen Douglas, the next President!"

Scattered cheering and handclapping followed this.

"Gee! Who'd have thought we were going to see the next President of the United States?" Henry said.

"Take a good look then, lad," said a distinguished appearing man with a white moustache and goatee, who was sitting behind them.

So Henry did take a good look. How stoutly Senator Douglas stood up there, how brave and grand for so short a man! The defiant way he held his great head erect and his chest out told you he had some lofty principle in mind, and in his massive chest the thunder of oratory to defend that principle. Henry began to feel afraid for Mr. Lincoln or anyone else who would oppose this doughty man. The Little Giant stood there awaiting his victim.

"If you're going to see the next President, it ain't that feller up there, Henry," Mr. Simms said.

Now a lusty roar broke out. People arose from the benches. It was the loudest human noise Henry, or anybody else there, had ever heard. But what was everybody so excited about?

"I swan if there ain't Uncle John Wolfe's Conestoga wagon!" Mr. Simms exclaimed.

It was a covered wagon, with broad wheels to ride well over the soft soil of the prairies. "It's the one he and his family come here in all the way from down in Pennsylvania, Bert!" Mr. Simms told the man next to him.

A magnificent team of six huge white horses drew it, driven by a rider with but a single rein. He was riding on the back of the nigh wheel horse.

"It's bringing Mr. Lincoln," Rufus shrieked, jumping up and down. "Say, no wonder your Douglas changed his mind about coming here in his fancy carriage!"

A tall man stepped from the wagon and onto the platform. Henry stared at him, hardly able to believe his eyes! It was the man who had called to him from the train! How lean and awkward-looking he was, though! Lank face, long dangling arms.

"There's Long Abe for you," Bert said.

"Looks like he's made up of nothing but shins and shanks and bony corners, don't he?" Mr. Simms laughed. "But just the same there he stands: Honest Old Abe!"

He wore the old stovepipe hat and a misshapen coat with sleeves far too short for him. His baggy trousers were so short they showed much of his rough boots.

What a difference between him and the Senator, who was richly dressed in ruffled shirt, dark blue coat with shiny buttons, light trousers, and polished shoes.

The immense clatter of everybody talking at once stopped only when a quartet began singing "America." Mr. Lincoln and Senator Douglas, along with everybody else, stood with the same respectful look on their faces. The song made everybody friends with the same feelings, and you wouldn't have guessed there was any argument among these people. Then they sang "Yankee Doodle." Eliza, Rufus and Henry sang together:

> "Fath'r and I went down to camp
>   Along with Captain Goodin',
>   And there we saw the men and boys
>   As thick as hasty puddin'—
>   Yankee Doodle, keep it up
>   Yankee Doodle dandy,—
>   Mind the music and the step,
>   And with the girls be handy."

After the singing and handclapping came a hush: the great battle was about to begin. There was a quiet feeling now within everybody. The big moment had come. All around him, Henry could hear people catching their breath, and he leaned his hands upon his knees to keep them from shaking.

Senator Douglas waited, looking cool and brave. From his dark eyes came a stare that would frighten you if you were his opponent, Henry thought. Mr. Lincoln, with his slightly stooped shoulders and his deep-set eyes, seemed sorrowful. He had a great loneliness in his face. Many of the people there had never seen him before. They thought they had never seen a taller and homelier man.

A man got up and introduced Abraham Lincoln to the people of Freeport. Then as Lincoln came forward, he towered above the audience and a great shouting and clapping arose.

"Yoweee!"

"Go it, Old Abe!"

He seemed so strong-boned and hard-muscled, you no longer felt he needed anybody to feel sorry for him.

"Fellow Citizens, Ladies and Gentlemen," he began.

"Hold on, Lincoln," a man behind him called. "You can't speak yet. Hitt ain't here."

Mr. Lincoln turned and said, "Ain't Hitt here? Where is he?"

"Here I am, Mr. Lincoln," a voice in the distance cried, "but I can't get through this crowd to the stand."

Then some strong men picked up the slender young man, lifting him into the air, and passed him along over the heads of the crowd to the platform.

"Bob Hitt is a shorthand reporter," Bert explained. "He's going to take down every word of this debate."

"For the newspapers to print," Mr. Simms added.

"Not only Freeport but the whole United States is listening to this," Henry said half to himself, half to the others.

"The whole world," Eliza said.

Now Abraham Lincoln was speaking. He had a high-pitched voice, but clear and sharp. Everybody could hear him, yet everybody listened hard. Every word was important.

First he told how Senator Douglas had given him some questions to answer. Then Mr. Lincoln answered the Douglas questions, one by one. They were about the slaves.

His answers showed that he never made any promises to any party just exactly how he'd vote. But he said he was "pledged to a belief in the *right* and *duty* of Congress to prohibit slavery in all the United States Territories."

"Sounds fine," Henry thought to himself, "but it's a lot better for the Territories to do their own freeing of the slaves. That's where Senator Douglas is smarter than you are, Mr. Lincoln!"

The gaunt giant now put *his* questions to the stubby little giant. They too were about slavery, especially in Kansas, which was not yet a State.

After each question, there were whistles and exclamations in the audience:

"Whew! *That's* a humdinger!"

"Douglas won't never be able to answer *that* one!"

The questions, written on a sheet of paper, were handed to the Senator. Everybody cheered.

"You know, Bert," Mr. Simms said, "that second question Abe put is the sticker. No matter which way Douglas answers it he'll be in hot water. What if a Territory wants to free its slaves before coming into the Union? Will you favor letting the slaves go free or not? If he says no, he won't let them go free, he'll have us against him for the Senate. If he says yes, let the Territories free their own slaves, he'll have all the slave states against him, and they're his main backing."

Henry hoped that the Senator would say yes, let any Territory free its own slaves if it wishes to.

"Doug'll answer that shikepoke plenty," a man behind them said.

"Shut up, you slaver," someone growled.

Henry decided that school fun wasn't shucks to a debate.

Mist and a fine drizzle drifted across the air occasionally, and gusts of chilly wind came with it, but no one seemed to mind. The show was too good.

As Mr. Lincoln went on speaking, Henry was glad that all the words were being taken down in shorthand so that his father and mother would be able to read them in the Freeport *Journal* the next week. But there was a lot to tell them that the reporter, busily writing the speech down but seeing nothing, would never get into shorthand and newspaper words.

Mr. Lincoln's words rang in the air like axe-blows, and Henry could imagine him swinging an axe with an easy sweep. Splitting big logs: making short work of it by taking long swings. His motions seemed no longer awkward but kind of graceful now, like those of a man at work who knows how to do it right. The people forgot how homely he looked. They only thought of what he said.

Sometimes he had the people laughing, but most of the time they were very serious. The noisy crowd was still now; all you could hear was Lincoln and the rustle of the wind in the trees. Even though the speech was difficult to follow point by point, you couldn't help listening to every syllable. It was like a kind of music. Now strong and angry, now strong and kindly.

Mr. Lincoln finished amidst deafening shouts and applause.

Henry was eager to see the Little Giant go into action. All around, he heard opinions sprout up:

"Now you just watch Douglas make the old scarecrow holler quits."

"Nope, Little Napoleon up there is as good as licked all ready."

Eliza turned to Henry and said, "I don't want folks to be slaves, do you?"

"No. I heard some men say today that Senator Douglas never claimed he stands for slavery."

"He does too," Rufus retorted.

"Sure he does," Eliza agreed with Rufus. "He looks down on colored people. You just wait and see!"

Henry didn't like to have Eliza on the opposite side from him, but he stuck to his views. "Shouldn't everybody have a chance to do their own choosing between right and wrong? We ought to let the folks in the territory of Kansas do their own deciding."

Now the famous Senator was introduced. The Douglas people sat tensely. They were fewer than the Lincoln people, but they knew their man was equal to Lincoln, no matter how good Lincoln was. Even the loyal Lincoln men on the platform looked on with respect as this great orator stepped forward.

He began speaking in the most cool and collected manner. The words came out in a rapid, even stream. Henry thought he sounded businesslike, practical.

The crowd waited anxiously for him to answer Lincoln's questions, and he did so with much vigor. As he completed each answer his supporters went wild with joy.

"That's giving it back to that backwoods politician!"

He answered the "sticker" question just as Henry hoped he would: by saying yes, it would be all right for a Territory to free its own slaves if it wanted to. But if it didn't want to, it would be all right *not* to free them either. Henry did not like this part so much.

Lincoln's melancholy face was undisturbed, but there was a little twist in his lips and a faint smile played around his mouth.

After a while Senator Douglas spoke louder and louder.

"Got the head and shoulders of a lion, and a lion's roar," Bert said.

This was the hoped-for thunder. The huge head now became very red, as though from the heat of the words coming out. He was so warm he took off his collar.

"Right sizable collar," Mr. Simms remarked. "It'd most go round your waist, eh Eliza?"

"Let him keep it around his big neck," Eliza said. "I wouldn't like to live in a slave State, would you, Henry?"

"No," Henry admitted.

Senator Douglas was every inch the great orator Henry had dreamed him, but somehow the glory was gone. The orator had an evil-looking scowl on him by now.

He criticized some Freeport people for treating a colored man as a friend. When the orator began calling people names, Henry could not make himself join in with the others and clap his hands.

Many people, though, seemed to think it was a fine speech.

A man shouted, "The railsplitter can't beat that!"

A fat man got up and shouted back, "You big galoot, watch Old Abe outsmart him!"

"He's done it already, Bert," Mr. Simms said. "Something very big has happened. Right up here in front of us."

"What?" Henry, Eliza and Rufus asked all at once.

"Well," Mr. Simms said, "you know how Douglas has been going around saying it's up to the people of each State to decide for themselves? So Old Abe asks him that sticker question: 'Are you for letting a Territory free all its slaves before it becomes a State?' Well, Douglas he has to say yes to that, else he knows *we* won't like it. But the slave-owners, they don't want *any* Territory or State to free the slaves. They'd have Douglas say no to that question. But Douglas he says yes. Now *they'll* never vote for him when he runs for President. His party will likely split up. It will never support him as a whole on those answers he gave."

"He's cooked his goose," Bert said. "He'll never be President. Hooray!"

"Old Abe's stopped him, right up here in front of us," Rufus exulted.

The Douglas men up on the platform seemed to realize this too. They looked worried and glum.

"Serves him right," Eliza said. "He doesn't care a snap if the Negro folks are slaves or not. Who wants a President like that?"

"You mean Senator Douglas doesn't care whether it's right or wrong?" Henry asked, trying to save one last shred of respect for his fallen hero.

"Not a bit," Eliza said.

"All Douglas cares about is politics," said her father firmly.

It was painful for Henry to learn this. But it seemed true. The speeches of both men had been full of political complications so you could hardly make out just where each man stood. Still, Lincoln had said at the very beginning he *believed* we should stop slavery, wherever we could. And Senator Douglas didn't say one word against slave-owning, not one word.

"Will Mr. Lincoln have a turn to answer Douglas's speech the way Douglas had to answer Lincoln's?" Henry wanted to know.

"Certainly," Mr. Simms said. "This is a fair debate."

All eyes were on Lincoln for his comeback at the Senator. Only a very few people there had any idea that Douglas had made a fatal mistake. Most of them thought he had won the day. Even some of the Lincoln backers were afraid he would not be able to refute the Little Giant.

The man's homeliness was there as much as ever, but it was a

good sort of homeliness, because it turned into kindness right before your eyes.

Henry studied the great sad face. It seemed to be sorrowful
with pity. Pity for all the suffering of the slaves.

"Whose business is it if a State wants to keep people in slavery?"
Henry argued silently along with Lincoln while listening to him.
"It's *everybody's* business everywhere. Isn't that so, Mr. Lincoln?"

". . . I repeat that I do not believe this government *can* endure
permanently half slave and half free . . ."

"Sure not," Henry thought as he listened. "How can we call
America a free country if it's only half free? That's right, Mr.
Lincoln!"

Lincoln finished with people on every hand crying to him, "Go
on, go on."

"I cannot, gentlemen," Lincoln replied; "my time has expired."

The cheering went on and on. Everybody seemed to be talking
at once; the grove was alive with chattering.

"Well, Seth, what yih make of it, heh?" someone asked.

And another answered, "Well, John, looks to me like Douglas
he was the best speaker all right, but I kind of thought Lincoln
told the truth best."

That was how Henry felt about it too. His head was so full of
thoughts that he had not noticed when Eliza and her father and
Rufus left.

People crowded to shake hands with the debaters. To shake
hands with Mr. Lincoln! Henry decided he wouldn't miss that for
anything!

He sat down again on the plank seat to wait for the crowd to
thin out around Lincoln. To others, Henry sitting there may have
looked very much alone, but he was not conscious of that. What he
thought of was that this fatherly man, "Old Abe," and he were
very close friends by now.

At last Henry got up and walked to the platform. A few people were still talking to Mr. Lincoln. At an opportune moment he touched the tall man's sleeve.

Mr. Lincoln turned around.

"Remember me, Mr. Lincoln?" Henry asked, looking up to the pleasant, lean face.

Mr. Lincoln smiled. "Have we met before, young man?"

"You called to me this morning from your train; I was in the buggy."

"So you're the boy with that fine spanking white horse," Mr. Lincoln laughed. He gave Henry his hand. It was a strong comfortable hand. "Glad to have a Douglas man come up to me like this," Mr. Lincoln said, still laughing, but very kindly. His gray eyes glanced down on Henry's chest.

Henry looked down at his jacket: he was still wearing the Douglas badge!

"Oh Mr. Lincoln!" Henry cried, snatching it off. "I forgot to take it off! I'm all for you now, sir!"

Everybody laughed, except Mr. Lincoln. Now he looked grave as he put his hand on Henry's shoulder and said, "Thank you. And will you tell me why you changed your mind?"

"Because I don't want slavery to spread. *All* the States and not just the new State should be worried about that."

Mr. Lincoln's face lit up. "If the boys and girls understand me that well this whole country will always be free."

As Henry walked up the street he could feel the grasp of that friendly hand.

The streets stayed crowded. It took some time to get the scattered wagon loads together. Soon they would all be winding their way homeward.

Grandpa Higgins was already holding the reins in the waiting buggy.

"What you all fired up for, Son?" he said.

"Grandpa, I've spoken with Abraham Lincoln!" Henry said, getting into the buggy and taking the reins. "He remembered seeing Prince from the train this morning. 'Fine, spanking white horse,' he said. Hear that, Prince!"

"I swan!" Grandpa said.

"Yes, and he shook hands with me too."

"You don't say! Here, let me shake the hand that shook Old Abe's." Grandpa took Henry's hand. "Henry Oaks," he said solemnly, "you've shook the hand that might yet set the slaves free."

As they drove out into the broad quiet prairie, Henry thought of the din he was leaving behind him. The roaring parades, crashing bands, and the booming voice of the Senator. But the warmhearted sound of Abraham Lincoln did not seem to be left back there; it seemed to be coming right along with Henry, within himself. "I've got so much to tell Ma and Pa," he said. "It feels just like I'm bringing Mr. Lincoln home with me."

Acknowledgment

The author and publisher wish to make acknowledgment of their indebtedness to the following publishers and authors:

B. J. Chute for permission to reprint "Archie and the April Fools."

Doubleday & Company, Inc., for permission to reprint "The Magic Ball" from *Tales From Silver Lands* by Charles J. Finger.

William Hall for permission to include "The Elegant Snoop."

Harcourt, Brace and Company, Inc., for permission to reprint "The Truce of the Wolf" from *The Truce of the Wolf and Other Tales of Old Italy* by Mary Gould Davis.

Harper & Brothers for permission to include "Gifts for the First Birthday" ("The Trapper's Tale") from *This Way to Christmas* by Ruth Sawyer; and "Thankful" by Mary E. Wilkins Freeman.

Holiday House for permission to reprint *Henry's Lincoln* by Louise Neyhart.

Houghton Mifflin Company for permission to reprint "The Peterkins Celebrate the Fourth of July" from *The Peterkin Papers* by Lucretia Hale.

Alfred A. Knopf, Inc. for permission to reprint "The Bunny Face" from *The Shoo-Fly Pie* by Mildred Jordan.

Charlotte Lohse for permission to reprint "Christmas in Summer."

Longmans, Green and Co., for permission to reprint "The Tinker and the Ghost" from *Three Golden Oranges and Other Spanish Folk Tales* by Ralph Steele Boggs and Mary Gould Davis; and "Candles at Midnight" from *Racing the Red Sail* by Alice Geer Kelsey.

G. P. Putnam's Sons for permission to reprint "Master of All Masters" from *English Fairy Tales* by Joseph Jacobs.

Story Parade for permission to reprint "Christmas Cherries" by Elizabeth Janet Gray; and "The General Did Wrong" by Jeanette Eaton.

The Viking Press for permission to reprint "The Peddler of Ballaghadereen" from *The Way of a Storyteller* by Ruth Sawyer.

Laura Ingalls Wilder for permission to reprint "Independence Day" from *Farmer Boy.*

A NOTE ON THE TYPE IN WHICH THIS BOOK IS SET

The text of this book is set in Caledonia, a Linotype face designed by W. A. Dwiggins. This type belongs to the family of printing types called "modern face" by printers —a term used to mark the change in style of type-letters that occurred about 1800. Caledonia borders on the general design of Scotch Modern, but is more freely drawn than that letter.

The book was composed by Kingsport Press, Inc., Kingsport, Tennessee, and printed and bound by H. Wolff, New York.